In the Absence of Ants

Kim L. Drake

For my two wonderful Babas

Anelia Drach

Justyna Duchak-Bedry

This book is dedicated to:

Those who have been diagnosed, or will be diagnosed with dementia, in its many complex forms; including Alzheimer's.

To the many physicians and scientists who work diligently to manage and cure this dreaded disease.

And to the spouses, children, sisters, brothers, relatives and friends, who spend countless days, months and years caring for loved ones.

While many are not able to articulate it… they thank you, and love you.

CONTENTS

FOREWARD

I chose to write this story because first and foremost, Alzheimer's is the scourge of our time, and the incidence of this devastating disease is rising sharply.

As of today, over half a million Canadians are living with dementia, with 25,000 new cases being diagnosed every year. By 2031, that number is expected to rise to a staggering, 937,000.

Worldwide, at least 44 million people are living with dementia; that's more than the total population of Canada, making this disease a global health crisis.

In this work, I have most humbly attempted to capture the difficulties one faces living with dementia, and in particular, Alzheimer's Disease.

In our story, In the Absence of Ants, you the reader will be privy to the many stages and emotions our central character goes through. You and only you are her confidant and have an upfront and personal seat with which to listen to the accounting of her journey, as told through narrative, memories and private dialogue. On some occasions, narrative and memories collide. This was done purposefully to allow a glimpse into the mind of our dementia-stricken heroine.

To a lesser degree, I involve her children, who share their struggles and doubts as they too navigate through their mother's illness.

This disease does not discriminate. It conscripts women and men of all races and colours, and although rare, it can begin as early as thirty. Therefore, I urge all of us to find ways to make a difference.

To that end, I pledge to donate half the royalties received to the Alzheimer's Society of Canada.

Together, we can make a difference!

Suffering, failure, loneliness, sorrow, discouragement, and death
will be part of your journey, but the Kingdom of God will conquer
all these horrors.
No evil can resist grace forever.

Brennan Manning

I'M SORRY

I'm sorry.

That's all she said.

Fine... she said more than that, but I'm sorry is something you say when you step on someone's foot or bump into a stranger at the supermarket. You say I'm sorry when you've forgotten someone's birthday, or arrive late to have coffee with a friend.

This required more than an awkward apology, devoid of expression. My God, she could barely look me in the eye; the energy of her discomfort practically bulldozed me out the door.

Wow. You do this for a living? Might be time to give up your day job.

She found time to stuff a bucket of brochures in my hand; and weren't they lovely, with pictures of a sweet grey-haired lady, surrounded by, presumably her children, all smiling? Was this supposed to make me, I don't know... hopeful?

Sixty-four years old and never had I endured such a pathetic expression of contrived compassion. It wreaked of pity; loathsome, and repugnant, and it oozed out of every crevice of her being.

I'm sorry. I'm sorry. I'm sorry. Blup, blup blup... the words kept erupting from her lips, like lava.

Oh, just give me the damn pamphlets and shut up!

I flushed as the humiliation and terror of it all, lurched my stomach into my mouth. Dread stabbed at my body, like a hammer pounding on a nail. My cheeks flushed; my saliva dehydrated, and my throat felt sticky and thick as if I'd swallowed a bag of quicksand.

Oh, God, I can't swallow. Don't throw up! Don't throw up; it will only add to the humiliation. Is she still talking over the pounding in my ears?

I heard myself say, thank you. Thank you? For what? A life sentence? The pamphlets? Ugh.

Have you ever paid attention to how our brains fill in awkward silences? We ramble. Words spew forth in a diarrheic stream, or ping-pong within the brain, ding, ding, ding. She kept apologizing, and I kept saying, thank you; we couldn't shut up.

Yes, and when we're not talking to somebody else, we're talking to ourselves, like we're doing right now. Yes, I'm proving our point.

Mutterings of appointments, specialists and who knows what else, was spoken as if from an abyss. All I could hear was the sound of blood bashing against my eardrums.

Oh, God... can't she say something comforting... something that eases the blow?

I grabbed the brochures of the smiling granny and left.

What did I expect, comfort, by an awkward hug, or limp hand on my shoulder, or would either of those gestures make an intolerable situation worse? Is it possible to make an unbearably unbearable situation even more unbearable?

What? Oh... clever.

By the time I left, I knew two things; I was fucked, and she was sorry.

THE OLD HOUSE ON NORTHCLIFFE

Bubbles float through dandelion parachutes; where silhouettes of winged creatures seem to hang in suspended animation. I watch them rise higher and higher, until, POP; they disappear like candy floss inside the Catalpa tree. Re-dipping my plastic wand, I blow again. The buoyant droplets float across the flower-laden fence. Pop! Pop! Pop!

Where do they go before they disappear into oblivion? Do they realize they existed? Am I here, mind, heart, body, and soul, or are soapy bubbles all that's left?

Boing! Boing! Bounce! Bounce. Up and down. Up and down. Baba lets me jump on the old mattress she keeps out in the backyard. Plop. Down I go, shading my eyes against the beams of light peeking through leaves, their backs twirling against the breeze.

Squirrels balancing on the buzzing wires precipitate more giggles than suspense. They traverse the braided

4

cords with comedic acrobatics. Run. Stop. Run. Stop. Turn. Go. Stop. Drop. Silly, confused squirrels.

Am I bird brained?

Cicadas snap their wings in the close breath of August; their rising hum vibrating through the floating dandelion fluff. Buzz, buzz… BuuUUZZZZZ.

You can't get me yet, you monster. I'm a little girl… a precious little girl. And she'll stay inside me forever; you can't get her. Cicadas will make you flee. They'll buzz you right out of there.

The orchestral symphony continues to play through the gauzy afternoon, echoing with strings of lilac and hydrangea, beetles and crickets. Butterflies in funereal motion, drift to the perfumed rosebush. Their fragile wings beat through the thick air; hwah, hwah.

You'll have to deal with me, and I'm no delicate butterfly! Oh, no. You may devour birds and bees, cicadas and squirrels, but you won't get me. You won't get me, not today. I'm still a child. You can't get a child.

Big fat honey bees move from lavender stem to lavender stem. Zzzz. Zzzz. As they collect pollen they're laden with heaviness. DZzzzzzz.

They don't falter by being weighed down. Oh no! They're not laden with sadness... It's a long, long road, but love? Love... will keep everything together.

I come close, but the bees ignore me. Work, work, work, buzz, zuzz, zzz.

What do you expect? We're Persona non grata. Some days, you don't recognize yourself. And you don't matter, you never did. Nothing in the universe cares about your existence if you don't matter.

I do matter. I do. You can ignore me all you like, and continue to carry out your heartless agenda, but I'm on to your devilry. You're trying to make me feel weak; defeated; but, you haven't come across the likes of me, you bastard.

When I was young, I used to be quite the force; always fighting some battle or other. No ignoring this girl, no sirree. Now, there's so little time...

So little time, but, I won't give up fighting windmills yet, I can't. Now comes the truest test. Yes, I need to be clever, shrewd. Brain not brawn for this foe. But, can I use my brain? Quite a conundrum.

I think you can.

Is that fact or opinion?

Does it matter?

I've always had strong opinions and I've never understood why that's considered a bad thing. Everyone has them; it's just, most people are cowards. They'd rather not have conflict. It takes guts to get off the fence; but in the end, opinions are just that; a notion, assessment, sometimes educated, sometimes not. But they're not forged in stone. One must have an open mind. It's essential for growth as a human being.

Is that what happened? I opened my mind and let you in? I thought being open-minded was a good thing, and now you're telling me it was a doorway for Satan Goo?

For instance, in my younger days, I was convinced I knew right from wrong; black from white; now everything's like a nondescript November. Age or disease? Who can tell? We all mellow and realize there's more shadow in the world than substance; less extreme and more middle. At least I have. If you've been paying attention, you realize that right and wrong are degrees of law and morals. However, some things have ultimate truths whether our perspectives allow us to see them or not; the earth is round; most stars are dead and gone even though we still see them and love never dies.

Revelations come with age or so "they," say. It's a trade-off - youth and idiocy for age and wisdom. Maturity brings less black and white, and more of an assortment of grays, like hair, and temperament. The skin turns sallow - okay, that's more yellow, but you understand what I'm getting at. While we gain a modicum of wisdom, we lose things too; the obvious ones being, childhood, inexperience, perky breasts... memories.

It's not impossible to see absolutes anymore, but it becomes more challenging, and rightfully so. We shouldn't cement our points of view into black or white; good or bad. Not everything is all in or all out; either-or - there's always, and both. Eventually, most of us come to live in the in-between spaces.

Did you ever watch ants? They march, march, march, work, work, work. Efficient, skillful. They attach themselves to the edges of sticky buds. Layer one peel, layer two peel; like the rhythm of a waltz. Tireless, symbiotic, never deterred. Are you aware that ants give us peonies? They're attracted to the nectar of the bud, and as they partake, the bud opens. Eh, voila, a blossomed peony. If ants didn't drink the nectar, the buds would get hard, lifeless... Dead.

Your brain is dead. Why the hell are you talking about ants? You were reliving a memory, and now you're back to the Demon Maestro; the orchestrator of the Symphony of Death!

Be quiet! I was contemplating how ants would stand up to the Great Devourer. Maybe the biters; you know, those little red bastards; they're small enough and tough! They'll eat up the hard stuff! Injection? Inhaler? Spray pump up the old shnaz? That's the ticket! Where was I?

Babcha squeezes my cheeks and kisses my face all over. She grabs my hands, and we step together step. Step together, step. Side to side, we slide through the grass in a music-less faux polka. She says that's how she and Dziadek do it at the Legion. They go every Saturday night, rain or shine, like clockwork... tick... tick... tick. Step together step. Faster Baba... faster. Round and round we spin; a kaleidoscope of white and brown checks blurs together like chocolate and marshmallow. I land breathless; the wind inside my tented dress expires like air farting from a balloon. I expect to go flitting around the yard, but instead, my dress comes to rest in an orderly grouping of squares. One square, two, three... four... five... too many to count, and little motivation.

I never noticed the paint before; the colour is washed up; washed out. The eaves are all cracked and hung askew. I must ask, David to fix that. Day vid? Is that right? It sounds odd. So many words look strange now.

Stop being dramatic. Words are just like that; they looked weird, even before our brain shrank.

Balls of grey and white fluff navigate through the blades of grass as if avoiding land mines. It's the first time; their mom has let them out. They're brave!

Am I brave? I want to be, but the cloaked Devil of Death is ready to scythe my brain in two. And, being brave doesn't mean you aren't afraid; it means being brave despite the fear. At least that's what, "they," say. This bullshit was invented by someone to entice soldiers into death.

Oh, bravo - you remembered some quote from years past. Good for you!

Don't be mean. We're in this together; we have to fight in tandem. Otherwise, we won't make it.

Mommy says we have to find the kittens homes.

"No, Mommy, no. I want to keep them. Pleeeeze? I'll take care of them. Pleeeze! Why? Why? Why can't I?"

Snowball, doesn't let her babies get far. She picks them up one by one by the scruff and carries them back to safer ground.

Do I have a safe ground? It used to be inside us, didn't it? Now, The Invader is occupying our territory, telling us what to do, what to think; what we can and can't remember…

"Babcha… come look at the ants."

ALL ABOARD!

I was never curious about "things."

How would you remember, brainless?

Some people love dismantling things. They remove screws, peruse components, split wires. A hobby, I guess. Well, "things" don't interest me; but people do, they always have. Guess Paige gets it from me - the apple and all that.

People are fascinating, aren't they? Some are cheery; others shy, sensitive; some, angry and spiteful. I don't judge. All of us have these emotions in different quantities. Still, there are those who seem to have more than their fair share of awfulness.

Is that a word - Ahhh full ness? Sounds nice, like something filled with awe. Why does it mean something horrible?

For instance, two kids brought up by the same two parents, living in the same house, attending the same school, eating the same food; one becomes a priest, the other a thief. Take my kids for instance; they're like night and day; one extroverted, the other like me; introvert-ambivert. How does that happen? It's a rhetorical question. I get it; it's complicated. Genius is not required to deduce kids who get beaten every day; or go hungry, will not do as well as their well-fed counterparts.

If you really want to study the human race, hang out in a bus station, or sit at the airport; these places are microcosms of life; joy, pain, tears, laughter. You see every emotion when people say hello or goodbye. These words are life in a nutshell.

What the hell are you talking about? Stay on topic. Are you talking about curiosity or kids?

My point is, I didn't have much time to fidget. I got married, and boom, boom, boom, three kids!

For those of you thinking about boarding the motherhood train, I'll let you in on a little secret; it's damn hard! Once those beings emerge, they're your responsibility forever and ever - Amen! And there's no vacation from motherhood. Oh sure, you can hit Cabo from time to time; it's mandatory for sanity, but the motherhood albatross is forever wrapped around your neck.

When hopes are dashed, does it break your heart? Cringe at disappointments?

Brought to you by the makers of Dice-em/Slice-em. What the hell was that? I sound like a hawker, for Cripes sakes!

Want a boy? You'll have a girl. Visions of candy floss clouds bobbing dreamily as the cherub slumbers? Colic! Idyllic expectations of being besties when they're grown-up and adulting? Nope - they've moved clear across the globe and never call. Worse? When they do call, they get on some jag about something that happened to them when they were eight, and how you're to blame.

Am I to blame? I did the best I could, didn't I?

Remember that Doris Day ditty? Will they be handsome, will they be rich, here's what she said to me... Que sera, sera... Will they be contributing members of society, or miserly and hateful? Who knows? You're only somewhat in charge because they arrive with their own personalities, don't they? Then life comes along with its wonderful lessons, and moulds, shapes, bends, and yes, even breaks them... and we break right along with them. Oh yes, you're the lucky participant in every heartbreak. Thank God for therapy!

Am I getting ahead of myself?

I have to rush, don't I? I can't lollygag; shrink, shrink, shrink... tick, tick, tick.

Sorry. I think I've exhausted what little patience I ever had on the damn kids. Let's backtrack a little.

Before the kid arrives, we should at least talk a little about pregnancy. Getting pregnant is the fun part, or at least it oughta be, but the nine months following can be hit or miss. I enjoyed being pregnant, but I know plenty of women who didn't. Temper those expectations! The not so fun part begins at labour and doesn't end till death do us part as they say. That's because, they're fed, changed, cuddled, rocked, walked, played with, sung to, and... wah. Lay them on their back... wah. Turn them over... Wahhh! Bundle them up, drive around in the car for hours... Wah! Sorry, that last one usually does the trick. Wah!

Here's a newsflash; when they cry, you cry... and the crying **never** ends. Never.

The first time they try to stand and come a breath away from taking their eye out on the corner of the coffee table; you cry. They break their arm, or leg (you're lucky if it isn't their neck,) you cry. When you see them doing stupid ass things like jumping off the garage, or sailing down some icy hill on a garbage can lid, you cry. When they come home from school crying after being called four eyes; get a zit on the day of the big dance; or a pretty girl stole the boy they like; you cry.

14

Then come the fevers, measles, chicken pox, mumps; and diseases you never knew existed, but your kid now has them. Anyway, you get my point. And that's only the stupid stuff. The serious stuff comes later, and you cry some more. I told you… never ends.

Now, it's their turn… oh, yes, the serious stuff is coming down the pike kids.

Don't cry kids… not for me.

You'll bear their pity too!

Oh, God, I can stand anything but that! Have you no mercy? You don't kill all at once with one swift stroke, do you? No, you're like Kudzu, choking and squeezing till there's no more breath, no more blood, no more brain!

It might sound as if I'm trying to dissuade you from boarding the Motherhood Train, but I'm not, because it all comes together; I promise. Love conquers all. Cliché, but true.

So, what if I said that already? It's not a crime to repeat oneself, is it? However, I should tell you, an assault on a brain is a crime! And you will pay.

Paige, my daughter, came into the world on a glorious autumn day, all six pounds, six ounces of her - not robust, but there she was, all blue eyes and smiles. I never asked the baby's sex, because I convinced myself I was having a boy; at least, I hoped. My grandmother told me girls were, (in her words,) a "pain in the neck." Translation? Girls suffer, grow boobs, have monthly visits from our, "friend," or as we can now say, periods; we give birth, cook, clean… and suffer, suffer, suffer - better to have boys. Never mind that boys cause a lot of our suffering.

The Many Ways Boys Hurt… Different tale for a different day.

Anyway, I found myself elated when the doctor said, it's a girl. A "she," was so unexpected; (remember that expectation thing?) It could have been the release of post-birth hormones or my relieved uterus, but there it was, unmistakable joy.

Soon, she'll be looking at me with those big doe eyes, and I'll be the baby. Will she be changing my diapers, or wiping away drool? Oh, baby girl, I'm not ready for you to be the mommy yet. Not yet!

Yup… all blue eyes and smiles! I named her Paige because I've always loved books. And if you're about to point out that Paige and page are different things; I've heard that once or twice. It's a homonym for Christ's sake. Don't worry, you're not the only one who doesn't approve. I got shit from both sides of the family, as neither side could pronounce her name. Pah-Je; Piegee? Come on people; it's not that hard! My advice? Go with a name you like. Your family will get used to it eventually, or create a hybrid of their own.

My grandparents weren't big on reading unless it was an article from their perspective ethnic newspapers. They weren't educated, and what schooling they had was not from books. However, every Saturday, my grandmother would ask me to sit with her and read the names from the obit section of the paper. It was more interesting than maudlin. However, there was always one name we recognized.

Personally, I find obituaries rather fascinating; the people thing again. Although, reading the details of people's lives often makes me feel inadequate. They never discuss a person's failures, do they? What's the deal? Johnny Doe, CEO, sailed around the world, never got lost at sea or life. Pfff!

But I digest.

Oh... That's not right, is it?

Brain blip. Ha-ha. Those two words look so similar, don't they? Digest-digress?

Sorry... I **was** talking about books, wasn't I?

When you can't afford that vacation in Cabo; and who can with a litter of kids? Pick up a book. I was Gone with the Wind, a wind that carried me to Wuthering Heights, and P.E.I. to the home of Anne of Green Gables. I kissed the Blarney Stone, sailed the South Sea; spent time in The Shack talking with God. I fought in the Great War, the French Revolution, and listened to tales by Don Quixote while being interrogated by the Spanish Inquisition.

I can't tell you how many times I fell in love in books. The Real Loves of My Life are chapters in - you guessed it, The Many Ways Boys Hurt.

Time is running out... for everything. Our time is running short, Fantine! I shall be miserable soon enough.

All I had to do was inhale the contents of the bound pages, and voilà; I escaped the dreary isolation of motherhood.

Can I be my own heroine? Oh, Rhett, save me from the brain fire - hurry Prissy, get the doctor before it's too late.

Was I reminiscing about motherhood?

A lousy thing happens when you talk to toddlers all day; you dumb down a little; become a little less interesting to big people.

I'm dumbing down now, aren't I? I'm no longer... adequate or interesting. But, it's not my fault! I've done nothing, and I accept no responsibility! You want me to blame my children for your brain eating? Not a chance! I'm placing blame right where it belongs. But, you don't care, do you? You keep chomping away, then shitting plaque like diarrhea.

And let me warn you; after all the time and effort poured into mommy-hood, "**I hate you! You're the worst mother ever!**" will be your reward. Yes. If these words don't echo throughout your brain, you haven't done your job; your thankless, wretched job.

My daughter would say I didn't support her. Why? Because she wanted to quit "Boring High," and go to Clown School. Imagine her surprise when I said an emphatic no to that? I also crushed her dream of being a Rockette - even though she was only five foot nothing; and, I didn't allow her to jump off a cliff because her friends were jumping. Sue me! She'd say I made her life such a mess, she became a therapist. Now, she tries to fix the rest of the broken world.

What about me, Paige? Can you fix me? Is there a philosophy, a therapy, a DIY book that can save me? I had a thought. If they could shove a toothbrush up there could they scrub it all away? You'll wonder where the plaque all went when you brush your brain with Pepsodent!

Paige does a lot of public speaking. She visits schools and talks to kids about drugs, bullying, and a variety of mental illnesses. I wonder if it scares the crap out of them? In my day, when someone came to talk to us about the dangers of drugs, the stoners laughed, but it scared me shitless. And that poster of the woman who looked like she was on meth with no teeth; the one that hung in every guidance office? She freaked me out too.

Maybe now's the time? Chew, snort, puff? So many choices.

Anyway, I don't think, Paige uses scare tactics, not that it matters. We're so desensitized to crime, violence, even death, we don't gasp at anything anymore. I blame T.V. News, which plays twenty-four/seven, on eighty-five different channels. You can't get away from it; disaster, famine, genocide, floods, drought; every day, all day. Holy crap!

Is that what broke my brain?

You know why your brain is shit, you just don't want to admit it. Denial is not just a river in Egypt.

As my grandmother used to say, "You people have everything from soup to nuts." She was right. There's so much information surrounding us, including what you read on, Faceplace... Oops, is it, Face... book? Anyway, not everything you read is true, is it? At least, Paige makes sure the kids have the right information. I'm proud of her for that. She's a salmon in today's fake news world.

Oh, I have all the information, don't I? Dementia; plaques clogging the brain; Alz.... No, no, no! No! I won't say your name; not now... not ever! I have to coexist with you, but I will not become your Stockholm Syndrome captive.

I only see my daughter a few times a year. Remember what I said earlier about them moving away? Just as well, Paige and I butt heads a lot; she'd be distant, even if she were here.

If I butted heads with the wall, would that scare the shit out of you; you big, brain bully? Would that confuse you, slow you down; shove you from the brain to the drain? I'm running out of options, and I won't bargain! There'll be none of this, God, if you get rid of the monster, I'll be a good girl. I'm already a good girl... aren't I? You can't bribe me with some cheap currency. And God doesn't bargain.

You don't care if I'm a good girl, do you? Good, bad, pain, comfort - it's all the same to you. Our little brains break down, and like a hooded demon, you spy and plot from your cloistered perch. No pity? Good! I hate pity. You're a major thorn in my flesh, like the one Paul endured. He was a good boy too once he stopped killing Christians, but even after he acquired good guy status, you left that stitch. Gentle reminder? So, is The Great Devourer my penance? It's hardly fair. I can't remember my evil deeds!

Oh, stop it; you know it doesn't work that way. Stop feeling sorry for yourself; you're not the only schmo with problems.

Mothers and daughters have interesting and complex relationships, don't they? Girls begin their lives wanting to be just like mom; then somewhere near their tweens, not so much like mom, and by the time they're teens, not at all like mom. I think they're afraid they won't develop that, je ne sais quoi that makes them... them. Don't worry, they grow out of it, but it takes copious amounts of patience, which explains why I have none.

Live for the moments when a phrase flies out of their mouth, and... wait for it... "Oh, shit, I sound like, Mom." Ha-ha-ha.

All aboard!

THE ALKA-SELTZER BOY

Three steps forward, one step back. Two steps forward, one step back, repeat. Repeat. Repeat. Rrrr, rrrr; the blades spin, then rest. Spin. Rest. Spin. Rest. Spin, spin. Rest. Mummy always cuts the grass on Saturday.

I'd consider a head thrust! Whirring blades; chop, and it's done!

Sticky pulp from a banana Popsicle slides down my thumb as I watch the blades of grass fly up and around the spinning metal; the sound rhythmic; mesmerizing. Rrrr, rrrr; rrrr, rrrr.

Does the grass know what's coming; that it's being cut down in its prime?

It must be such a relief when death is expeditious. No time to spiral, or over think; no fretting or anxiety. You clutch your chest, grab your head; a split second of pain

23

and down you go. Heart attack, brain aneurysm; it's tough on the families and friends, but Paradise for the deceased.

You don't operate like this, do you? That would be too kind. Minute by minute, hour by hour, day by day, week by week, month by month and so on, and so on, and so on, like that annoying shampoo commercial; you take us down one brain cell at a time. No respite! Tick, tick, tick goes life; tick, tick, ticking until death is the only thing you can think about; until you can't think at all.

"Mom, Angela's outside. Can I go over? Please! Can I? Can I?"

"All right, but come home for supper! No eating over there."

"Okay."

Angela's my best friend. I eat there all the time. Her mom makes the best spaghetti ever, but she only speaks Italian, so I've learned how to say, si grazie; that means, yes please, and grazie, which means thank you. They're almost the same, except one has a si, in front. I know lots of Italian words. Mangiare, sta 'zito, and culo. Don't use that last one.

Anyway, I haven't eaten here since, Rosanna got hit by a car - that's Angela's baby sister. We were playing out front when Rosie chased her ball onto the street, and a car drove right over her head. Angela's mom was screaming and crying, all at the same time. The ambulance came, and the whole neighbourhood watched as Rosie was whisked to the hospital.

They'll be doing that with me too, won't they? Gathering, tsking, pitying.

Angela was crying really hard too because she was supposed to be watching Rosie; but her mom didn't care, she kept yelling and screaming at her, and hitting her on the bum. Mummy said, "See… that's why you never run onto the street."

It wasn't Angela's fault. It was good Rosie didn't die, but Angie's mother was sad after that… forever.

They'll be sad for me too, but I hope not forever.

Flying down the driveway, a heat mirage rising from the concrete chevrons, pursues me like an exhaled breath. I'm running too fast; can't make the turn… Ouch! A branch from the front yard hedge digs into my shoulder, but it doesn't matter, I gotta go. Angela got a pink hula-hoop today.

Inertia propels the circular disk, around and around. I watch it spin, making a whirring sound as it brushes against the pleats of her skirt. Angela always wears skirts; her mom says that's what girls are supposed to do.

Mummy says it's almost 1960, and girls can wear whatever they want, even pants.

"Let **me** try!"

I thrust my hips forward and back, gyrating as fast as I can, but the pink plastic sphere slows, slides, then dies in the grass. Again, and again, I attempt what for me feels like the impossible. Spin, fall, die. Spin, fall, die; repeat, repeat, repeat.

Like my brain; spin, die; spin, die.

I hate hula-hoops. They're stupid!

"Let's get the trike!"

The wheels make a gudunk, gudunk, gudunk, sound on the sidewalk as we ride up Northcliffe. I like to stand on the back with my hands on Angela's shoulders. My foot pushes off the pavement and propels the trike forward.

"Faster, Angela! Faster! Peddle! Go!"

Thirty-nine, forty-one, forty-three.

"Go, Angela! Peddle!"

Forty-five, forty-seven, forty-nine, fifty-one. Bobby Sidorchuk's. Time to turn around. I'm not allowed to go past Bobby's house. One time, I rode to the top of the street, and around the corner. When I started back home, the street was long and scary, and I couldn't see my house anymore. It was like being on the moon. I had nightmares over and over after that; it was night, and The Alka-Seltzer boy was chasing me down the dark, empty street. I kept running and running, but I couldn't get home.

"Mummy! Mummy!"

"It's okay… you're having a bad dream."

"No, no… he's here."

"Who's here?"

"The Alka-Seltzer boy. He's chasing me. I'm supposed to be home when the street lights come on, but I can't because…

"Okay. It's just a nightmare… Shhh… go to sleep. I'm right here."

"Don't leave me, Mummy."

"I won't. Shhh… You're safe… everything's okay."

I push like mad even though we're going downhill.

I'm going downhill, aren't I; downhill in an uphill battle? Oh, the irony. Does that make sense? Wait! Dammit! Let me figure

27

it out. Uphill battle - downhill spiral? Yes! It makes perfect
sense, right?

One-more-PUSH and… Both elbows hit the ground like
anvils. The bike and Angela are crushing my chest. Tears
explode! Blood pours from under weeping skin, turning
the linen concrete a scarlet red. The hanging flesh is dying;
already turning purple and black. Pebbles embedded in
the bone, sting and burn. I run home, through blinding
tears. Ouch… stupid branch!

Mummy! Wahhhhhh! Wahhhh! Mummy!

"What's the matter?"

"I…. I…. wah… I…"

"All right, take a breath. Calm down. Calm down. What
happened?"

"I was pushing Angela, and… and… the bike… it… it…
tipped over and…

"Okay. You're all right. Let's have a look."

"Owwww!"

"I haven't done anything yet, silly girl!"

"Don't touch it! Mummy, no!"

"I have to use the tweezers to pick out the little stones. Sit still; this might hurt a little."

"Owww! No! Stop!"

"Keep still!"

"Owww! What's that?"

"It's Bactine."

"NO! It'll sting!"

"It won't sting, I promise, and it will make it stop hurting. Hey, look, Snowball's got a kitten in her mouth."

"I don't care! Owwww!"

"Almost done… There! We'll leave the bandages on for a few days."

"Why are you laughing at me?"

"Because, it looks like you fell into a big bowl of chocolate. Wanna see?"

Mucky tears streak my cheeks, and the brown and white squares on my dress, are now a bloody eggplant.

"Mummy, my dress is all dirty."

"It's all right; we'll throw it in the laundry! Come on, let's wash up."

The warm cloth glides across my face, sweeping the hair back from my forehead.

"Better?"

I nod.

"Mummy, it hurts."

"I know, sweetheart."

DON'T COOK EGGS IN YOUR HOUSECOAT

"Hello, I'm Dr. Adair. How can I help you today?"

"It was a ridiculous accident. I didn't sleep well last night, and I was too tired to dress, so I slipped my housecoat over my p.j.'s and started breakfast. The sleeve of my robe was hanging down, and whoosh."

"Okay, let's have a look. Ooh, that's a nice burn. How's your pain level on a scale of one to ten?

"It's not bad."

"On a scale of one to ten?"

"Um… seven?"

"We'll get salve on that right away, and bandage you up. That's the thing about burns; once we cover the nerve endings, the pain goes away. There's already a fair bit of blistering, so there's a possibility of scarring."

Lucky I'm not vain. What's one more battle scar?

"I'll get the nurse to give you something for the pain. Be right back."

"David, why don't you grab a coffee? I may be here a while."

"It's okay, Ma, I don't mind."

"I'd rather you… Oh! That was quick."

"Yup, we're pretty organized around here."

"This shot is for the pain. Any allergies?"

"No."

"Are you on any medications?"

No, no, no, no, no! Oh, shit!

"Excuse me. David… can you please get me some water? I feel parched."

"Is this your son?"

"Uh-huh."

"Okay. David, there's a water pitcher on the nurse's desk just around the corner."

"Thanks. Be right back, Ma."

"No hurry."

"Meds?"

"Uh, right… let me get my list. Can you hand me my purse, please? Uh… where is… that thing? Ah, here it is. So, Lunesta; sometimes I have trouble sleeping, Memantine and Lorazepam."

"When were you diagnosed?"

"Ouch!"

"Oops, Sorry."

"Not long ago. My son doesn't know, so can we please keep this confidential?"

"Almost done… there. The doctor would like to speak with you. Sit tight."

"I'm fine though."

"Here's your water, Ma. Are you ready to go?"

"Not just yet. Oh, here comes the doctor. David, can I get some more water, please?"

"Sure."

"So, the diagnosis of Alz…

"**Was recently**. But, as I said to the nurse, I haven't told my son, David, yet."

"And you're seeing… uh… Dr. Bennett?"

"Yes."

"You realize, this is a very serious condition."

"Yes, of course, but I'm still trying to wrap my head around it."

"It's important you share this information with your family. You need support."

"Right. I'm aware."

"Who's your O.T.?"

"Who?"

"The Occupational Therapist? Ah… Ms. Velasquez? You'll like her."

"Mm-huh."

"Okay, good. I'll forward this report to Dr. Bennett. You should be aware that an accident can speed things up; it's a shock to your body, so please discuss your diagnosis with your family as soon as possible."

"Here, Ma. Discuss what?"

"Oh, just how to change the bandages, and what antibiotics I'm getting."

"Mr.?"

"It's, David."

"David, would you mind stepping out, I'd like to examine your mom a little further."

"Oh... sure. Is everything okay?"

"Everything's fine; just want to be thorough."

"Ma, I'll wait for you in the coffee shop."

"Fine. I'll come get you when I'm done, David."

"We shouldn't be much longer."

"No problem."

"… When is your next appointment with Dr. Bennett?"

"Off the top of my head… um… sorry, can't remember, but I have it written down at home."

"I suggest you tell your son in the meantime, so he can be present."

"Yes, I will."

Talk about beating a dead horse, for fuck sakes. I'll tell my son when I'm damn well ready. You assume you know what's best for me - but you don't. The lunatic hasn't taken over the asylum yet. I'm still in charge, you pompous ass.

"You need to change the bandage at least once a day; here's a fact sheet on that; oh, and try not to get your arm wet."

"How do I take a shower?"

"Try a bath. Is there someone who can help you wrap it in plastic or something before you get in?"

"Yes, my daughter-in-law, and, if she's busy, my son will do it. He's a good boy!"

"I can see that!"

"Here's a prescription for Erythromycin cream, and Tylenol Threes. Take them only as needed. I'd also like you to make a follow-up appointment with your family physician, just to be sure the arm is healing. Any green pus, excessive swelling or fever, return to the E.R. immediately."

"Okay."

Codeine? Excellent! Maybe I'll become an addict. God forbid I forget about The Great Devourer for a few hours!

*Oh, sarcasm; that's new. Anyway, don't rush; forgetting will happen soon enough. It's the plaque monster's mandate! But... do I want to forget **anything**? Even "it?" Yes. No! Oh God, I don't know. Awareness of the beast means the brain's still working, right?*

"Go home and rest. Remember, your body's had a shock."

Shock? He doesn't have a clue! How about finding out there's a monster living in your head, eating your brain? This? This is a piece of cake!

"It will take two to three weeks for your arm to heal. Remember... If the blisters don't appear to be healing or you have any other concerns, come back to emergency. Here's my card. While I can't divulge this information to your family, I urge you to discuss your diagnosis with them. This disease can progress quickly; it's important to have a strong support system. Good Luck!"

Again? *He must think I'm an idiot. I don't seem to be the only one with memory issues. Wait, did he repeat the instructions because of my diagnosis? Oh, God... how humiliating. And, good luck? Are you shitting me? Ugh. That's almost as bad as, I'm sorry.*

Concerns? I'm guessing he meant over the burns, although he wasn't specific. I figure if we talk about other things, I could bend his ear back about a year and a half!

The worst part of this was having to phone David and bother him at work. Okay, fine; the **worst** part was the humiliation of setting myself on fire. That's what I get for cooking eggs in a housecoat with sleeves like a monk's robe.

Idiot! Moron! If you weren't so lazy, none of this would have happened. And don't complain, you don't deserve sympathy.

"Are you okay, Ma?"

"It smarts a little, but, I'll be fine."

"Well, the doctor wrote you a prescription for painkillers."

"Yes, David, I'm aware. I was there."

"Sorry, Ma."

"That **just** happened, David; like three minutes ago."

Shit, even I can remember that.

I'M SHOCKED

"I'll drop you off at home, Ma, and scoot over to the pharmacy."

Can you get me salve for my bruised ego?

Never mind your stupid ego. What about not seeing the flames till our arm started sizzling?

You aren't telling me anything I don't know. I was there! Anyway, it's a good sign you're still talking; I'm still talking - that we're talking to each other? Is there a difference? I am just talking to myself, right? Or is it The Nasty A; deceiving, manipulating?

What's the code word? No! No! Don't speak it, not even inside my head. Nod if you still remember. The KGB of brain disease, has his cup to the wall, listening to every word... Shhh.

"David... my elbows!"

"What's wrong with them?"

"They're hurting."

"What? You said it was your arm. Didn't the doctor examine you?"

Shit! Why did I say that?

"No... no. I... I... didn't. I didn't! Look... my elbows are fine."

"Are you sure?"

"Yes. See? Nothing."

"Ma, what the hell is that?"

"These? These are scars from when I fell off a tricycle many moons ago."

"I never noticed that before. Is it hurting?"

"No, and I'm sorry, David. For a second it felt like there was something wrong, but it's probably the pain from the burn radiating up my arm."

"Phew. Good. Anyway, you're home. Remember what the doctor said... relax, okay? Make some tea and lie down."

"You want me to lie down with a hot cup of tea? That's a recipe for another disaster. Ha-ha-ha."

"Hilarious. You know what I mean!"

"Sorry, I was trying to infuse levity into the situation. I'm fine. Go!"

"Should I get you settled first?"

"That's unnecessary, David!"

"Are you sure?"

"I'm positive. I'm fine, now, get going. I'm looking forward to the codeine. Wild times. Ha-ha-ha. Oh, and don't forget the cream… **And** the tape."

"Anything else?"

"A chocolate bar?"

"A chocolate bar?"

"Told you… wild, ha-ha. Now go."

Where do kids get that they're qualified to parent their parent? It's school, isn't it, the university years, when they assume they know everything about adulting? Or, does it coincide with the time children become mommies or daddies? They begin caring for their spouse, their kids, pay taxes, make car payments, so why not lump mom in there too; nice and tidy. I've got news for them; four years of theoretical learning is a drop in the bucket compared to sixty years of practical life experience. But, it's more than that - there's something innate about a mother caring for a child. It's easier for magnetic north and south to flip polarities than it is for a mother to reverse roles with her kids. Wait. Doesn't that happen all the time? Maybe a more accurate example would be like a leopard trying to change its spots? Well, you know what I'm getting at.

Parenting grown-ups is a lot different from parenting children. For instance, I can stay out late, eat what I please, when I please; go to bed at nine and sleep until noon. I don't have to play well with others, or share, and I don't have to be nice. Also, I can't be grounded. We grown-ups are a handful, aren't we? One of the other perks of adulthood is being able to parent ourselves.

*Maybe the kids **should** practice. Like it or not, they'll be parenting you soon, and themselves, forever after.*

*No, I'm the parent! **I'm** the mom! Me! I won't relinquish that right; not yet, you bastard. You'll have to tear it from my cold brainless hands.*

"Okay, Ma. That wasn't too bad. Got your pills, your cream, the tape, and a Coffee Crisp."

"By the way... how on earth did I ever get along before you and Paige were here to boss me around? I've seen you both through chicken pox, measles, mumps, fevers, flu, colds, rashes, bites; **and** I recall one or two sleepless nights

43

in Emerg. Remember the time you fell on that plastic toy soldier, and it got impaled in your chin? That was four stitches. And what about Paige's appendectomy? Remember that?"

"Okay. Do I have to remind you it was me who drove to the drug store to get all this? How about, thank you?"

Now he's teaching us manners?

"What brought this on?"

"I'm sick and tired of being treated like a child."

"What are you talking about, Ma? I've never treated you like a child. I'm just looking out for you. And Paige never had her appendix out."

"Are you sure?"

"Yeah. I think I'd remember that."

Oh, shit, then who was it? Was it… me? I'm slipping. Must be the accident; the stupid, careless accident! I'm not focused; not paying attention. I must have singed my brain too.

"Anyway, David, the point is, I'm more than capable of looking after myself."

"Of course you are, I only meant...

44

"Uh-huh. Let me hobble over to the couch."

"Pouting doesn't become you, Ma. What's going on? Hello? I see… now you're giving me the silent treatment? Didn't you just say, you weren't a child?"

"Time for you to go."

"Okay. Are you sure you're, all right? I'm serious now."

"Yes, but I'm tired. I guess setting myself ablaze took it out of me. I'm sorry. Thank you for everything, and I'm sorry you had to leave work."

"No problem. I'll work tonight. Don't give me that look, Ma, I love what I do. Rest. If you need anything, call us. Meg said she'd stop by tomorrow to change your bandage."

"Okay. Give me a kiss."

"Are you sure you're all right here by yourself?"

"Goodnight, David."

"Goodnight, Ma."

"And, thank you."

I'm not a helpless, senile invalid, not yet, dammit!

Where the hell's the kettle?

INFLAMMATION

Where was I? Oh yes, kids.

David, my youngest, ran half marathons in utero, and like a UFC fighter, kicked his way into the world, six weeks early, putting me through the worst back labour a human has ever endured. He then spent the following fifteen months doing nothing. No exaggeration. He didn't roll over, crawl, sit, smile or cry. I was convinced he'd incurred brain damage during the delivery, or had that weird disease; the one when you can't feel pain? What baby doesn't cry when they're hungry? He ate fine when I fed him, but otherwise, he ignored his hunger pangs?

Didn't his little tummy rumble? Poor baby.

Oh, you should talk!

You're right. I may be hungry right now for all I know. Hmm. Are we all born with dormant brain disease; camouflaged, hunched in the trenches, waiting for the day, the enemy waltzes in with its goo-goo gun and sprays goo-goo bullets all over? It doesn't matter, because even if you're prepared, there's no halting this enemy; no infiltrating its secrets; no decoding its message.

So... growing in leaps and bounds, which was not a good thing, because, at fourteen dead weight months, I could barely carry him. The kid refused to walk. I'd put him on the floor, and he'd sit there, like one of those clown punching bags; only twice as serious.

When he wasn't dead awake, he was dead asleep. He'd go to bed at seven, sleep until seven in the morning, eat, go back down at ten, sleep until noon, wake, eat, back to the crib at three, wake for dinner, and start the cycle all over again.

It would thrill most parents if they had a child who ate, slept and never cried, but my concern was becoming panic, as my almost fifteen-month-old was behaving more like a zombie than a toddler.

I wonder if he will feel the same way about me? Don't panic, sweetheart, it's just a little brain inflammation.

A pediatrician's parade ensued, with each saying the same thing; he's perfectly healthy, just lazy. **Lazy?** Can a baby be lazy? Whatever the case, at fifteen months the kid leapt to his feet, took off running, and just like that, was as normal as any kid; which is like saying snow in July is normal. All kids are weird.

By three, he was speaking in full sentences, and if I'd dressed him in a suit, he could have been, Alex P. Keaton!

I said he didn't cry, but there was that terrible year his legs were growing. Poor tyke! It was as if he was being drawn and quartered. I spent every night of that miserable year, rubbing, warming and weeping. The doctor suggested I alternate heat and ice on the sprouting bones, and dose him with good old-fashioned, Tylenol.

"Don't worry," he said. "He'll **grow** out of it."

Puns? Really? Not funny!

Inflammation is all the rage now, isn't it? Depression? Inflammation! Stomachache? Inflammation! Ingrown toenail? Inflammation!

The brain plague from hell? Inflammation! Hey, that one may be true. If that's the case, let's throw a bucket of ice in there and see what happens, shall we? I could stick my head in the freezer and pray my eyeballs don't freeze before Señor Death's do?

Life boils down to four things, the first two being, stress and inflammation; which cause high blood pressure, stroke, heart attack, cancer, depression, psychoses, and a host of other ailments. The other two as I've already mentioned are hello and goodbye. Hello, inflammation, goodbye body. We don't stand a chance.

How realistic is it to think we can dodge stress? And what's the point of telling us stress kills if we can't avoid it? It's not like being able to give up cheese and alcohol; God forbid. Might as well resign ourselves to the fact one of the above **will** kill us.

There's mounting evidence that inflammation even causes… Alz… brain disease.

Sorry, am I off topic?

Anyway, the kid survived. In fact, both progenies made it through their childhood with little or no brain damage; which is miraculous given all the tumbles, scrapes and falls - teen years included. Success!

I didn't say I survived without brain damage! It's possible that parenting teens broke my brain!

That's funny; right?

Yeah… hilarious!

HELLO?

"Hello?"

"**Hello**! I've been trying to reach you for weeks Where have you been?"

"Who's this?"

"It's been so long you've forgotten the sound of your best friend's voice?"

"Oh, Jean. Hi."

"Hi yourself. I've called at least ten times this month. I even stopped by... twice. Where're you been? I've been worried sick."

"Sorry. I should have called, but with David's new job, and Meg's schedule, I've been crazy busy. You know how it is... Gramma duty."

"Lots of people are asking about you; Sarah, Betty, Margaret. Mary said she's called too. We thought you were sick."

"Aww, that's sweet, but I'm fine. Please say hello to everyone for me."

"Oh, before I forget, Leslie asked me when you were coming back to choir."

"Who?"

"Leslie, our choir conductor?"

"Sorry, I didn't hear you for a second. Oh, Jean... I'm bowing out of choir, at least for this year. I've got so much on my plate, I can't manage it all. Would you mind passing that along?"

"Are you sure? We're starting rehearsals on the Christmas Cantata this week. Who will sing in my ear and keep me in tune?"

"Ha-ha, you'll manage, I'm sure!"

"Are you sure everything's okay?"

"Yes, fine."

"It's time you got a cell phone. It is 2018."

"I have a cell phone, Jean. David bought it for me, last year."

"What's the number?"

"Same as the house phone."

"So, why the hell don't you ever answer the damn thing?"

"It's such a bother. Half the time I forget to charge it, and when it's in my purse, I never hear the damn thing ringing."

"What about voice mail?"

"I have no idea... but listen, Jean, to be honest, I'm not getting much out of church these days. It's hard to sit in those rock-hard pews, and I'm not crazy about the new Minister; he's a bit of a droner. Don't you find him boring?"

"He's no, Reverend John, but then again, who is? We were lucky to have John for all those years, but we have to give the new guy a chance. He'll get better once the nerves settle down."

"I'm not as sure about that as you. I fell asleep during one of his sermons. If Joyce hadn't poked me, I would have fallen out of the bloody pew! How embarrassing would that have been?"

"Ha-ha-ha. Well, aside from Minister Mike, what about the U.C.W.L.? Christmas bazaar prep is coming up; you love that, and then there's the luncheon at Valleyfield Villa. Plus, on December fifth, the women's group is singing for the Alzheimer's floor at the hospital. You could sing with us for that, couldn't you?"

No! No! No! We couldn't. No!

"Jean… the truth is, my heart isn't in it anymore. I'm churched out! Paige calls it, burn out? We've both done our due; it's time for the younger ones to take over. Plus, I'm finding it hard to stand **and** sit these days; it's my hip."

"What does the doctor say?"

As if I need to see another fucking doctor!

"She always says the same thing; not bad enough for surgery, blah, blah, blah. Yeah? Well, it's bad enough to keep me awake all night. Bloody doctors!"

"Why didn't you tell me?"

"God, if I complained about everything that bothered me; reflux, plantar fasciitis, arthritis, thinning hair, failing eyesight, and things that shouldn't be mentioned in polite company, that's all I'd ever talk about. That's what's great about the grandkids, they youth us up. Ha-ha."

"Well, lube helps with the unmentionable; ha-ha, but what about food or a lift to the…

"No! I don't need a thing, Jean. Thanks. Meg takes care of all that for me."

"You haven't given up on Euchre too, have you? I'm happy to pick you up."

"Sorry, Jean. I know I sound like an old poop, but I'm so tired after spending time with Raine, by the time I get home, I crawl straight into bed."

"Why do I get the feeling there's something you're not telling me? You don't sound like yourself. Tell me the truth; are you depressed?"

"No, of course not! Really. I'm fine, Jean, just busy."

"Well, if Mohamed won't come to the mountain… How about a coffee date? We can chat. Does Wednesday work?

"Um, let's see. Sorry, Jean, no can do. I'm at Raine's school; she's in a play."

"In the middle of the day?"

"Yes, a show and tell thing."

"Okay, how about Thursday?"

"I'm sorry, but this week is out."

"If I didn't know you better, I'd say you were trying to avoid me. You aren't upset with me, are you? Did I do something?"

"No, don't be silly."

Can you please just leave me the hell alone?

"Are you sure? We've known each other too long to be coy, so if you're mad at me, you should say so."

"Ha-ha. I'm not mad at you, Jean! Look, as soon as my schedule frees up I'll call you, and we'll get together, okay? Say hi to everybody at church for me."

"All right, but I'm going to hold you to that coffee date."

"Okay, Jean. Talk to you later… Bye."

Jean Tarchuk and I have known each other for over forty years. She's one of those women who can take it and dish it out; a straight shooter, like me. We've only had one significant disagreement, and it was when she thought I'd divulged a confidence. It was a terrible misunderstanding. Turns out someone overheard our conversation and blabbed. I was off the hook, but those two weeks were hell.

Jean is what you call, salt of the earth. There's nothing I can't talk to her about... We've been each other's best friends since the moment we met. We just clicked. Gosh, we've had a few adventures. We travelled together; married the same year and were each other's Maids of Honour. We were pregnant together and raised our kids together. We've shared every joy, sorrow, and every roller-coaster moment life threw at us.

I've thought about telling her... you know... but I'd need to tell the kids first, and the chances of that happening are slight to none.

I could tell her... I should. She'd keep it to herself. This is Jean we're talking about. She wouldn't blab. I can trust her, can't I? But, what if she mentions it to David or Paige by mistake, or lets it slip at church? Too many choir gossips.

What did Reverend John used to say? The devil comes in through the choir loft? I can't chance it.

Sorry, my friend, there are some adventures we can't share.

I HAVE A STOMACH BRAIN?

Damn stove!

Yeah, it was the damn stove; not the brain gaps.

Must you remind me of this every minute of every day? You're like a nail gun on a two by four.

My God, the house could have burned down. What the hell was I doing, stirring a pot in a housecoat with sleeves like a bloody choir robe? Ugh! I'm such an idiot!

Did I talk about this already? Sorry.

Paige says, I shouldn't call myself names, because it's bad for the psyche, and she's right. Every nasty comment goes to our cells; it's like punching ourselves in the gut, over and over.

Have you heard the latest? "They," say our stomachs have brains. It's true. I watched this BBC News report, that said we have over one hundred million little brain cells lining the stomach, along with gobs of bacteria. The more good bacteria, the less chance of depression or anxiety. This lends credence to the ditty... nobody loves me, everybody hates me. I'm going to the garden to eat worms.

Does this mean, I might be able to shit you out my ass? I'll **need** *a stomach brain once my head brain is a prune.*

Well, I'm not an idiot. I've been witty on occasion. I'm well read, a good conversationalist; someone who can hold their own with most anyone. A raconteur should be conversant on a variety of subjects. It's less about brains and more about acquiring knowledge.

Thank God. But, what good is all this accumulated knowledge if it's all disappearing? I'm losing... everything, even useless memories.

You can learn a lot playing games like Trivial Pursuit, for instance. It's brilliant for amassing trivia. Duh! Chess is real brain food, but requires a great deal of patience, and as I may have mentioned, I've run short. But, between them all, Scrabble is my favourite. I've always loved the written word. In fact, I fancy myself quite the word... word... Well, damn, that's embarrassing. How ironic. The point being, I... uh... Sorry, lost my train of thought.

Yeah, that train left the station a while ago. Remember when we were able to complete a thought or finish a sentence? Good Times! ...Day after day, all cleverness, fading... fading. Oh, God, my stomach brain is churning. Let's not get ourselves worked up. Breathe... Again... Again... Once more. Okay... okay. I'm okay.

What was I saying about a word? Dammit! A word... word? Come on! Ugh.

Cooking was also something I liked when I remembered recipes; not that I followed many. I would whip up a dish with whatever was in the cupboard. Now, reading words confuses me. Three eggs, sift the flour, add vanilla and stir. Okay. Three eggs what? Sift? What? Sift? Yes, sift. What? It's enough to give you whiplash. Does this happen to everyone our age? Don't answer that.

Yes, yes it does, but...

But what? You think in our case, The Brain Shrinker has something to do with it?

Well, of course, it has something to do with it, you idiot!

Stop calling me an idiot! I forget, that's all. And it's not my fault.

After what I refer to as, the burn "incident," I haven't used the stove, period. To be honest, I've lost interest.

Is this because Miss Smarty-Pants swings by and checks on us like the Gestapo? Come veet me; you left stove on!

Fine! I get it; I f o r g e t!

Anyway, moving on. Have I told you about my crazy dreams? I read about it in one of those pamphlets the apologist gave me.

Did you know some people experience super vivid dreams with the Cannibal Menace? Like, last night for instance; I dreamed I fell into a kaleidoscope and kept spiralling downward until I landed on a carousel pony. As I spun faster and faster, coloured lights pierced through me, like shards of broken glass. Musical notes were dancing to the En Bee Cee tones. It sounded as if the peacock swallowed a calliope. I was... Exhilarated... Intoxicated... Frightened... Confused...

Is dreaming in colour, supposed to make me feel better? A gift from you know who? Beware the Trojan horse; it's filled with goo. And whether it's coloured or sepia is irrelevant. Don't let dreams suck us into la-la land. Colour is overrated.

Maybe when the brain is dying, it yearns for the bright colours of life, like excitement, joy; the lustiness of health? Days are washed out of late, sepia-toned, nuanced gray; a perpetual twilight. How ironic... Twilight is my favourite time of day.

Life is filled with irony. Is this true in general, or just my truth? Have I always been stonewashed, or is my brain being caulked; covered in cataracts? Dreams and reality are melding; assimilating each other, making it difficult to distinguish between the two. I wish I could remember more of what I was going in the present.

Going? Is that right? Is right the opposite of left? Does it also mean… correct? Same spelling? Ugh! Work, damn it!

Not going! Doing! Doing… Sorry.

Stop gas-lighting me. I'm NOT stupid! I'm not! Just because I mix up words doesn't make me imbecilic! Does it? Oh, no you don't, you bastard, you won't make me cry! I'm not brainless yet. Oh, God, you're exhausting!

Another thing that happens after fifty? Words on the tip of the tongue, melt like cotton candy; thoughts corkscrew; confidence descends into waffling uncertainty… The mind is sucked into a hellish vortex of confusion, and… Sorry, that was a bit Cussler-ish.

Come on. This is no ordinary ageing thing. We know who's eating me alive… Chomp… Chomp. And would Hannibal Lecter Menace enjoy a glass of Chianti with my brain?

Word… word … Wordsmith! That's it!

JINGLY DANGLY THINGS

"Hey, Mum, it's Meg. What's the matter?"

Oh, shit. What does little Miss Perfect want?

"Nothing."

"Really? You seem upset?"

"Well, I am… uh… I can't find my, uh…

Stay calm! Stay calm. Don't panic! Breathe.

"Bandages?"

"No."

"Ointment? Tape?"

"No!"

"Painkillers?"

"NO!"

Oh, God. Leave!

"Mum, are you in pain? Are you hurt?"

"No, nothing like that."

"What is it then?"

"I've lost something."

"Oh, okay. Well, whatever it is, I'm sure we'll find it."

"I'm looking for the uh... the... the dangly things?"

"Dangly things?"

"The... jingly, dangly things. Dammit!"

Stay calm, or the entire family will descend on us like the plagues in Egypt.

"Try not to upset yourself, Mum. Sit down for a second."

Great! Sure! That'll help.

"I don't want to sit down, Meg!"

*Behave! Control yourself, and whatever you do, **don't cry!***

"Please, Mum, sit... for a moment."

"I DON'T WANT TO SIT DOWN, Meg!"

"All right, Mum. All right… Take a deep breath. We'll sort it out, hmm? That's it… Now, tell me again… take your time."

Why won't she go! Fuck!

"I need groceries and…

"And these things are at the store?"

No, you stupid moron! The things aren't AT the store. I need them to GET there!

"NO, Meg. Let me finish!"

"I'm sorry. Clearly, I'm not helping."

No shit, Sherlock! Don't treat me like a two-year-old! Now she'll call David. We're doomed. Dammit, I can't bother him anymore this week! We can do this. Calm down!

"Those things, Meg? They're for the car."

"Keys?"

"Yes! **Hallelujah! Thank you!** That's it; my keys. I left them in the dish by the door, and now they're gone! Someone stole them."

"Why would anyone steal your keys, Mum?"

"How should I know? If they aren't there, and no one took them, where the hell are they?"

Smarty Pants!

"They probably fell behind the table, let's have a boo, hmm? The rad? Shoot, I don't see them, but did you know the answering machine is unplugged?"

"What?"

"Yup… let me just…

"It's fine, Meghan! **Just leave it alone!**"

"Mum, there's ten messages here. No wonder you didn't return my call. One of these messages is from me. I called to see if you needed anything at the drug store."

"I don't care, Meg!"

"But, Mum, some of these messages may be important. You should listen to them."

"I SAID NO! Mind your own fucking business! If you must know, the phone was ringing off the hook, so I unplugged it! Can we stick to looking for the damn keys? Please!"

My head is about to explode. Bonus! It would save Brain Basher the trouble.

"Are you upset over something that happened at church, or…

"UGH… No, Meg. I want to find my keys that's all. I don't want to talk about my answering machine, messages, or any other damn thing. Help me, or leave!"

"Okay… sure… Did you check your purse?"

"Of, course I checked my purse, Meghan; I'm not an idiot; and the coffee table, and the bedroom dresser; the kitchen, the bathroom, under the couch, and everywhere else in this bloody house! I'm telling you, somebody stole them!"

"Look. It's obvious you're upset, Mum, but please stop yelling at me. Let me check the garage, maybe you left them in the car?"

Where the hell could they be? It's that damn neighbour! She took them, I just know it!

"The car's here mom, so I doubt anyone stole the keys. Please don't get exasperated. I hear your frustration, and contrary to how it seems, I **am** trying to help."

That's not proof. She took them to steal the car later.

"Well, you're not!"

"Mum… I think you should forget about this for now. You're too upset to look at the moment. Tell me what you need, and I'll swing by the grocery on my way to pick up Raine from school."

"**Please,** don't bother. You have enough on your plate."

"It's no bother, I promise. I need some stuff too."

Yeah, sure she does. Better give little Miss P a list, or she'll never leave.

"Well, if it's truly no bother."

"Nope. And please try not to worry about your keys, they'll turn up."

"Meg… I'm sorry, I shouldn't yell at you!"

"It's all right, Mum. I'll be back later with the groceries and to change your bandage. In the meantime, make yourself a cup of tea and relax."

Why is everyone suddenly plying me with tea? Will Earl Grey find my keys? No? How about Mr. Rooibos? How could I lose my keys? **Stupid! Stupid! Stupid!**

Easy... you have a rotting, shrinking, brain!

Shut-up, before I bash you in with a crowbar.

Without keys, how will I get to church? How will I see my friends?

What friends?

What do you mean? I have friends! I must have. Shit, even Hitler had friends! Oh, Jesus... Oh, God, I can't remember them; not a single one. Think! Focus, dammit! I'm warning you, you son of a bitch; I will bash my head in, and end this right now.

Okay... breathe. In and out... that's right. Rule number one...

And what about Mrs.... Mrs. Who? I'm sure I visit someone. Wait... where? Where do I go? The Hospital? St. Luke's? Where are they? No one? So, I'm useless as the saying goes, like tits on a bull?

You 're the sick one now. You're the one they'll visit.

Oh, God...

CALVARY IS COMING

"It's okay. Shhh. You have to nap; all babies do. You'll be safe here. See, warm and cozy. I'll be back after your nap."

Mew. Me-ew.

"Shhh! Go to sleep, or there'll be no playtime later."

Mew. Mee-ee-ee. Meow.

"That's enough of that!"

Jump… Stair… Jump… Stair… Jump… Stair. Landing. When I lean on one foot, then the other, the stairs make this noise; listen… Reeek… creak… reek. Do you hear it? Baba says it's because "hause ees old." House is old, la la la. I'm not supposed to play up here, la la la, 'cause I could fall - hmm mmm mmm.

I'm the bossy boss princess.

"Hey! You down there! Yes, you! Fix this staircase at once! Do you hear? I'm Princess La-dee-da, and my father is King of the land. You shall do as I say, Miss Snowball, or I shall imprison you, and turn your head into a coconut!"

"Meow. Meow. Meeeow."

Our screen door has a million, zillion holes. I tried counting them once, but I only know my numbers to ten.

Next year, I'm going to kindergarten, like a big girl. Mummy says school is fun, but we went there once, and it was full of bossy boss teachers pretending to be nice.

Anyway, when the door closes, the decoration in the middle goes BANG. Baba says, "keep screen dor clos, and don slam," but I can't help it; I forget.

One time, a big wasp was flying around the kitchen, and Baba got mad at me.

"You see, now wasp een hause because you naht clos dor."

She killed it, and I cried.

"Why you cry?"

"It wasn't his fault I left the door open. He wasn't doing anything wrong."

"Eef I not kill, he gonna bite you. You keep dor clos, and he not cahming in."

She sounds funny when she talks in English. Oops… someone must have left the screen door open because a fly is crawling up the banister… Oh-oh, it flew into the kitchen. Baba's gonna be mad. I don't care if she kills a fly, they're a nuisance.

I wish she could kill you, brain eater! You're a nuisance too.

I like to pretend the railing is a big pole, inside a castle. I climb off before the end, because once I hit the big ball at the bottom and hurt my, pee-pee. Another time, I fell off and smashed my knee.

Hey, my crayons! I like colouring, but I don't colour when Mummy's around, 'cause she makes me stay inside the lines. She says it's important to be neat. Mummy's a bossy boss too.

*Oh, Mummy...life **is** messy!*

What's your favourite colour? Mine is blue. The brown one looks like number two. Hey, that rhymes. La, la la… Hmm, hmm, hm; hm, hm, hm, hm, hm, hm, hm. Purple… blue… I don't like white, and if you do we'll have a fight.

'Cause it is waxy, and the colour doesn't show... on the paper here below. Hee-hee-hee Hey... like wax paper? See? I, don't need to go to bossy boss school, I'm smart already.

"Are you playing on the stairs?"

"No."

"Are you sure?"

"Yes."

"You know what happens when you lie? You get spanked once for misbehaving, and spanked again for fibbing."

"I'm **not fibbing!** Look, Mummy, I drew you a picture."

"Very nice. You did a good job staying inside the lines."

"Thaaaank U."

"Honey, have you seen the kittens?"

"No."

"Are you sure? I'm a little worried. I can't find them anywhere?"

"Well... they could be napping."

"And where would that be?"

"Don't worry, Mummy; I made a nice bed for them and covered them with a blanket."

"Where?"

"In the sock drawer."

"Honey, the kittens, can't breathe in there, and Snowball's upset. She's crying because she can't find her babies.

Remember how upset you were when you lost your jingly things?

Did you find them, Mummy? I can't remember. Mummy, am I still your baby? Can you find me? Please, Mummy, I'm lost.

Oh, God in heaven, I said I wouldn't bargain, but if you take away the Plaque Prince, I'll do whatever you ask. Please Lord, I've been kind. I fed the hungry, clothed the poor. What more can you ask of me?

*What kind of God allows evil to take up residence in someone's brain? Why didn't you stop it? You threw Satan out of heaven; you destroyed **your** enemies, how about mine; or is New Testament God hands off? Didn't you send, Jesus? He healed, didn't he? You keep telling me he's still around; **well, where is he?***

Then again, you let them torture and nail your son to a cross, so what chance do I have? Substitutionary atonement? Nah. Never bought into it. I still don't understand why you did it, and I don't care why you did it! Jesus, you're still my Superstar!

*You understand you didn't **give** me this monster, but you can take it away. Please, Lord, I beg you; do it for my children. If you do, I'll shout from the rooftops - MIRACLE! MIRACLE! I'm healed! I'll give you all the credit.*

You won't though, will you? Why? Why won't you give me a miracle? Am I so worthless; so undeserving? Where is your mercy?

What happens when I get so far gone I can't remember you? What if you send an angel and I can't recognize it? If I forget who you are, will you still take me to heaven? Jesus, remember me when you come into your kingdom.

I know the cavalry won't save me from Calvary, will it?

I didn't think so...

PENANCE?

Maybe they're wrong. The brain's like a peony isn't it; full of folds and layers all squished like a bud? What if they inject me with ants? They'd open the folds. Part of my brain was breakfast, but before the Menace Muncher gets to lunch, can we please try ants?

I'm sure by now my scrawny daughter-in-law has blabbed the whole story to David, which means David's called Paige. The last thing I need is a lecture, especially from my daughter. Ugh! Don't misunderstand me. I love Meghan, but she's a little dramatic for a psychotherapist.

Sorry. Did I say, Meg? I meant, Paige. She's the psychotherapist, but it's tiny Ms. M who's the problem! I'm sure she's already made a mountain out of a molehill, and all because I was a little upset over losing my keys. Okay, okay, I was perturbed, but aren't I entitled to be bummed without the Mounties showing up? Lately, I've been feeling as if I'm not allowed to be anything but happy; which is upsetting in itself given my circumstances?

Who are you kidding? You aren't capable of happiness anymore...maybe never were.

Calm down, Mum. Take a breath, Mum. It'll be all right, Mum. Let's be positive; think good thoughts, everything will work out; always look for the silver lining, the rainbow, the fucking pot of gold! Ugh. She's a nerve grater. Has anyone ever calmed down after being told to calm down?

There's a natural flow to life; happy, sad, high, low. You can visit Oz, but you can't live over the rainbow. As enchanting as Nirvana seems, it's not real.

David met Meghan in the eighties... or was it the nineties? Well, it doesn't matter. I remember the first time I met her. At a smidge over five feet, she looked like a ventriloquist's puppet, with a Howdy Doody smile, and protruding eyes. She's **always** smiling, even when she's ticked. In fact, the more miffed, the bigger the smile. It's... unnerving. I'm making her sound awful, but she's actually attractive in a deer in the headlights sort of way. It's just that smile!

I'd never met anyone like her, until I met her mother. Oh, Lord, how did that woman not develop lockjaw? And that...look of amusement was the least annoying thing about her. The most irritating, was the constant repetition. She was like the drunk you can't shake at the party. Smile. Blather. Belch. Smile. Repeat… Vomit.

From the moment she arrived, she'd start, "I have to be home at five. Is it five? Nanna and I bake biscuits. I like baking. Is it five?"

"I don't know Cookie."

"I have to bake biscuits at five. Is it five?"

"**I don't know, Cookie!**"

"Did you know I bake with my Nanna?"

As we're fond of saying in my family, I can't hear that story one more time!

That's when I started calling her, Kooky Cookie.

What, and you don't repeat yourself?

Do I? Like That? Kill me now.

Meghan's father was out of the picture before David and Meghan met. They said he died of cancer, but I'm betting Kooky Cookie talked him to death, all the while smiling! One day, she up and wandered away. Two days later, a neighbour found her half frozen in a field, laying in dog crap. That was near the end.

Death could have done her a favour that day, but he let The Brain Eater devour her instead. Oh, the irony, having the same disease as the smiler-blatherer. Have I mentioned how life is full of ironies? Anyway, it must have jumped from her into me, like lice. Karma? Perhaps.

My recollections of Cookie may sound cruel; I mean, it's not as if she could help being annoying, what with the, Alz... dementia and all, but geez. And it's not that I didn't like her because she sounded like a broken record, or because she looked like Howdy Doody Senior. There's something to the adage of eyes being the window to the soul, and hers was a little... Grinchy.

Is it a crime not to like someone? Don't imply this is my penance. And just because someone is sick, or grins, or is blind or demented, doesn't automatically make them all sugar and spice, does it? She wasn't all that nice.

I'm nice, aren't I? Kind, considerate, empathetic? I must be. I cried through every bloody Disney Movie. Remember when Bambi's mother died in the fire? They asked my mother to leave the theatre because I was hysterical. And what about Dumbo? I sobbed for days. My God, I cried through; Up! Up, for God's sake!

You son of a bitch! You gobble up humanity. Is that what you did to Cookie? I'm sorry, Cookie... I didn't know.

Cookie died right after David and Paige were married.

Wait… What? God help me! Ugh, stupid, stupid brain! Shhh. Let me think. David and… and um…

I meant to say, David and **Meghan.**

Poor Cookie.

*Poor **me**. I'm now, Kooky Cookie…*

Just when I think I'm still in charge, a useless memory tumbles out of the old noggin' like dice on a craps table. At this moment, I'm coherent, but lately, there's a better chance that the house boss takes over, and who knows what nonsensical card he'll pull from the deck? Mad ramblings? Tongue-tied stuttering? I guess it'll be a surprise! Have I mentioned I hate surprises?

Of all the things I **want** to remember, Kooky Cookie isn't even at the bottom of the hit parade, but, "Mr. Go Fuck Yourself," doesn't gobble the back-shelf memories; apparently too far to trudge. Lazy bastard.

I keep trying to stage a coup, but even when I'm in lockdown, this prisoner is not ready to accept her life sentence. Not yet.

I DIDN'T PUT THEM THERE

One of the great joys of my life is my granddaughter, Raine; chestnut curls like Judy Garland, hazel eyes like her daddy. When I see that precious face, all my anxieties and fears disperse. Even Goo-Brain withdraws. She's a blessing; a second chance at having the relationship I always hoped I'd have with my daughter, Paige. Is that wrong? Isn't that what grandchildren are for, enjoying all the perks of parenthood, without parental responsibilities? Grandchildren allow us to by-pass parental faux pas and enjoy, indulge and spoil.

In hindsight, I see the detours; places where the Paige train changed tracks; when the conductor fell asleep, not because she didn't care, but because she was too damn exhausted to stay awake. And the farther that car chugged from the main line, the more difficult it was to get it back to the designated station.

That's my way of saying, I screwed up. Oh, not with the big stuff, but with the million little things, like being too tired to listen, or thinking that thirteen-year-old's problems weren't as big as my own. But you can't complete the puzzle when pieces are missing, can you? And I'm tired of beating myself up. No one's perfect. I did the best I could; at least that's what I tell myself. Even the Betty Crockers of the world ask for re-dos, occasionally.

Doubt, guilt, second-guessing; isn't it all part and parcel of the motherhood whole? We can always do better, but, as the old song says, it takes two, baby. What Paige and I have is a showdown, except she didn't show.

There's a risk opening old wounds; hurt feelings; perhaps expanding the chasm? She gave up, let go, moved on, but I refuse to give up on battles of old. Once upon a time, there was a Berlin Wall, a no foreigners clause in the Forbidden City, and no blacks were allowed in the front of the bus. If **they** can make peace why can't we?

In the meantime, while I wait not so patiently for a heart wrenching reckoning, Raine continues to fill my soul with unconditional love.

And now you're stealing my second chance, you bastard.

That's right! Enjoy it while you can, because it will be gone soon - all of it - her face, giggles... all of it.

Raine, or Paige?

Both.

Stop… I can't bear it!

"Hi, my beautiful girl! Ooooh, you give the best hugs."

"Gramma, are you crying?"

"No, sweetheart, I have something in my eye."

"I came to help Mommy fix your bandage."

"You did? That's very nice. Maybe someday you'll grow up to be a doctor."

"I want to do what Auntie Paige does when I grow up."

"You do? That's wonderful. You're already an excellent helper. How was school today?"

"School was good. We had art; that's my favourite class."

"I know. Did you do anything special?"

"Yup. Hold on. It's in my back pack."

"She's getting so big, Meg. I wish I could be around to see her grow up."

"I know. Too fast. Are you planning on going somewhere?"

"No. It's just that at my age, anything can happen."

"Oh, Mum. Don't be a gloomy Gus. Think positive thoughts. Sixty is the new forty!"

Ugh. Does anyone have a hammer?

"Gramma… this is for you. Do you know what it is?"

"Hmm… Well, it looks like… keys?"

"Yes! I painted them for you, 'cause Mommy said you lost yours. Is that why you're crying?"

"No, honey, I'm crying because you are the sweetest more precious girl in the entire world. I'm gonna kiss you all over. Mwah, mwah, mwah, mwah, mwah."

"Tee-hee-hee."

"Gramma, did you find your keys?"

"No. Wanna help me look?"

"Uh-huh. Do they look like my drawing?"

"Almost. There's two silver ones and a teeny-weeny gold one."

"What's the teeny-weeny one for?"

"The mailbox. They're all tied up together with a big red ribbon. Where do you want to start, hmm?"

"Can I start in the kitchen, I'm thirsty."

"Sure, you can. Let me lift you up...

"Uh-uh. I can do it myself. I have to climb on a stool at school, to get things from my cubby."

"Okay, but be careful."

"I will."

"Meg. Thanks so much for going to the grocery for me, and I'm sorry about earlier. I shouldn't have shouted at you. Really, it's myself I'm angry with. I simply can't imagine what happened to those damn things."

"They'll turn up. But, I understand how maddening it is to lose things!"

"Your arm is healing well. How does it feel?"

"A little stiff."

"I'll put more cream, that should help."

"Did you schedule your follow-up with the doctor?"

"I didn't bother. Do you think I should?"

"Probably. All right, let's wind this around, and…

"Meg… I really do appreciate the things you do, especially for David and Raine. It's difficult being a busy mom; I remember the days. So, you don't have to nurse me, and I'm also capable of running my own errands and…

"Gramma? Look what I found?"

"Let's have a look. Well, I'll be. Where were they?"

"In the cupboard with the glasses."

"Mommy! Mommy! I found Gramma's keys!"

"How in the world did they get in there?

I didn't put them there! Did I?

Of course, you did, you twit!

How? When? I need to slow down; take time… make notes. Isn't that what the pamphlet said? Make notes and post them around the house?

You're such an idiot! Won't that tip them off?

Oh, it will. God, I can't think anymore! I used to be so clear headed, didn't I? Anyway, how will notes help? Why did I suggest that? How is singing going to help me remember? Oh, God, everything's getting mixed up again.

Now, Meghan will tell David, and David will tell Paige, and here come those plagues!

I can do this. I once was lost, and now, I'm...

No, hon - you're just lost.

THE SHIT STORM BEGINS

"How was, Ma?"

"She was... agitated, but, we found her keys; well, Raine found them."

"Okay, so why was she still upset?"

"A carry-over? I'm not sure. David... your Mum is having issues."

"What do you mean?"

"We found the keys...

"Yeah, you said that already."

"In the cupboard."

"So?"

"This is how things started with my mom, remember? She lost things; mumbled to herself, was aggressive. Remember the time she slapped me? These are signs, David."

"Oh, come on Meg. Ma opened the cupboard to put groceries in, probably had the keys in her hand, and dropped them in there by mistake. That could happen to anybody."

"The keys were with the glasses, David, not in the pantry."

"Okay, so, she was getting a drink of water or juice, and dropped them. What's the big deal?"

"It's not just that. She's also been acting a little, off. Sometimes, she's irritable; like when I bent down to see if her keys had fallen behind the rad, I noticed her answering machine was unplugged? When I tried to plug it in, she told me to fuck off and mind my own business."

"What? Oh, come on, Meg, really? She didn't slap you, did she? Ha-ha."

"This isn't a joke, David."

"And she actually told you, to fuck off... in those words?"

"No, but she told me to mind my own business. And when's the last time you ever heard your mother use the "F" word?

"Quite often, actually, but only when you're not around."

"I see. Okay, fine. Anyway, I tried to let it go because I realized she was torn up, but it rattled me. She apologized later, but still."

"Okay... So?"

"Seriously, David. I've never seen your mum so agitated; and when we came back with groceries, she was crying."

"Are you sure?"

"I think I know what crying looks like, David."

"Did you ask her what was wrong?"

"Raine asked her, and she lied. She said she had something in her eye."

"Maybe she did."

"David, if you aren't going to take me seriously...

"You're reading way too much into this, Meg. I remember you went through some of these things with your mother, but don't jump to conclusions. It's natural for someone Ma's age to misplace things, or forget stuff. Hell, I do it now."

"David, you aren't listening. It's more than that. I'd love to be wrong about this, but we'd better keep a closer eye; and by we, I mean all of us."

"You **mean,** Paige?"

"David, I love your Mum, and I don't mind looking in on her, but it's important for Paige to take responsibility too. At the very least she should be aware of what's going on. Plus, this is her field of expertise."

"So, you want her to play doctor?"

"I'm just saying she knows a lot about this kind of stuff. You should run some of these things by her and see what she says."

"Meg, Paige's career involves a lot of travelling; you know that. I won't lay a guilt trip on her just because Ma left keys in some cupboard!"

"And what about **your** career, David? I'm glad it's taking off, but with you working late most nights, it puts all the responsibility on my shoulders. I'm the one that chauffeurs Raine to art class, dance recitals, play gigs, does your mother's shopping, changes her dressing; and at the risk of sounding selfish, I'd like time to myself occasionally. As I said, I don't mind checking on her, but I can't be your mother's primary caregiver."

"Whoa! Whoa! Who said anything about caregiving? You act as if she's incapacitated and needs to be admitted to a nursing home or something. The woman misplaced her keys, and you're having her committed? Christ, Meg, isn't she allowed to be distracted?"

"Sure. And the mumbling, the anger?"

"What... talking to herself? Thinking out loud? We all do that."

"Do you think she's been to the doctor recently?"

"What? How the hell should I know? I don't even know when your check-up is."

"Was."

"See?"

"Well, perhaps you should find out."

"How, Sherlock?"

"Broach the subject. There's nothing wrong with showing concern, is there?"

"Hey, Ma, when's the last time you were at the doctor, because Meg thinks you're losing your mind?"

"Oh, come on, David. Don't be obtuse!"

"What the hell does that mean?"

"It means slow on the uptake, stubborn ass."

"Forget it, Meg, asking Ma about seeing the doctor out of the blue would sound suspicious. Then she'd ask, why I'm asking, and what would I say?"

"It might open a dialogue?"

"About what?"

"David, you're a jerk."

"You see? We all say hurtful things when we're upset."

"Really? That's your answer? I'm concerned about your mother, and you're trying to prove a stupid point? You've gotta be kidding me. Are you trying to pick a fight? If you need to blow off steam, go to the gym."

"Sorry. Look. I know this is bothering you, so, if it makes you feel better, I'll pay closer attention from now on; I promise. If she behaves abnormally I'll, 'broach' the subject. Now, will you please let it go?"

"And Paige?"

"No! I won't involve her, unless there's more to this than, Ma losing her stupid car keys, and using the word, fuck. Ha-ha."

"Still think that's funny?"

"A little."

"Not involving your sister is a big mistake, David."

"If it is, it's my mistake."

"Fine. From now on, **you** check on your mother. Her bandage needs changing once a day - at least for the next week. She's not comfortable driving because her arm still hurts, so you can take her to the doctor's for her follow-up on the tenth; I made the appointment yesterday. Don't forget about groceries, she likes to go on Thursday. Oh, and several over-due books need to go back to the library, and…

"I get it, Meg. You want me to be more involved. Fine. I'll take Ma shopping on Thursday, and to the doctor, but I'm not comfortable changing her arm thingy."

"Thank you, David. Juggling all these tasks isn't easy. Besides, this will give you a chance to spend quality time with your mother. It might even be a stepping stone to some difficult conversations."

"I won't ask her anything personal."

"You may not have to."

I AM NOT PARANOID!

Soon, they'll be talking about me; whispering, conspiring; glancing at me out of the corner of their eye. They'll smile, but not with kindness; with pity, the strain that makes me invoke rule number one; that's my no crying rule.

They'll dissect and discuss; compare and, confer.

"Did you, psst, psst, psst - I hear her brain's - cluck, cluck, cluck. Bok, bok, bok."

People think they're being discreet when they gossip behind someone's back, but they're not. Ms. Cancer and Cousin Heart Failure aren't stupid, they can sense the suppressed tones; trace the pity stench. It's how I know my next-door neighbour is spying on me. She's stealing my cheques.

She does it to infuriate me; she also put my car keys on the shelf with the glasses, but Raine was too smart for the old cow.

In the middle of the night, when she thinks I'm sleeping, she comes and kills my flowers. I can smell the poison seeping through the window, suffocating me in my sleep. God forbid a dandelion waft over and defile her yard. She better stay away from me; I have more than a damn dandelion infection.

The reason we know we're being talked about is that communication is ninety percent nonverbal. Humans are adept at reading body language, and we're not deaf, so knock it off with the whispering.

We get it, we're part of the Diseased and Dying Club. We don't need help feeling excluded or shunned.

Woo-hoo, we're in on your little secret.

Hooray for you, asshole.

Years ago, I had an uncle who was dying of cancer. We all shushed each other, and donned perfect sympathy smiles before we came into his room. Nobody wanted to mention the C word, as if speaking it would hasten his departure. News flash - you can't make a person sicker by talking about the fact they're dying; all that does is rob them of the chance to have closure. People "in the chute," as a friend of mine used to say, are well aware of the fact that they've got one foot out the door.

I admit, not everyone wants to discuss their demise, but it's mainly because **other** people get uncomfortable. We do everything in our culture to avoid the word. So, and so, passed on, is sleeping, breathed their last, is at peace, gone to rest, home with the angels. We keep our children as far away from death as we can, as if it will rub off; taint them. But we can't stave off the inevitable.

It's unpleasant, I get it, but wouldn't it be better if we prepared ourselves instead of pretending we can escape? It's no wonder the subject terrifies us.

When I was a kid, everyone went to funerals. Kids asked questions like, why is the body cold, why does his face look plasticky? Grown-ups didn't shy away from talking about the tough stuff.

And funerals were communal. Just as family and friends gathered for births, they also congregated to mourn the dead. But, we don't have funerals anymore, do we? Bodies are whisked away, buried, burned, kept out of sight. No more paying respects at the funeral home; too uncomfortable. We don't know how to act, or what to say. Instead, we have memorials, gatherings even parties where the deceased isn't even mentioned. It's small talk over cocktails. Ugh. In my opinion that's worse than a funeral. It's sad. Anyway, avoiding the inevitable is futile.

When I die, I'm not going to have my family hire wailers or anything; and please, no platitudes like, "heaven needed another angel," (as if they'd say that… ha-ha,) or, "at least she's out of her misery." While it might be true, these sentiments don't help the family. I just want people to be able to express their grief, to cry, share stories. And, I hope my neighbour has to stand there and stare at my cold dead face. Ha-ha-ha.

Remember the television show, I've Got A Secret? Every week a contestant would come on the show with a secret, and through a series of questions, the panel had to guess what the secret was. Well, I've got a doozie, but it's my secret to tell, and when I share it, I don't want anyone talking behind my back.

You're a bloody hypocrite!

No, I'm not. My situation is different. I'm not lying in a hospital bed, where the only thing my family has to do is visit. If I tell them I have you know what, it would force them into taking me to appointments; picking up medications, supervising, cleaning, cooking, and suddenly, I'm no longer, mom, I'm burden number one.

So… this is about burdening them?

Yes! And… it's unnatural! I'm their mother! You don't ask a child to parent, a parent. Ever!

Honey, you won't remember!

I might remember; not everything, but, something. Besides, Brain Shrinker shouldn't be center stage. He's not the star of the show.

So, this is about ego?

No. No! It's about not burdening the kids. I could live another ten years, and you want me to spill my guts now?

But your brain might be viable for only another two?

Thanks for the encouragement. Aren't you supposed to be my ally in this; my partner in crime? And what a heist it is… stealing memories. I won't make my kids accessories! Besides, if I say nothing, he's Persona non grata; stuck in the shadows where he belongs.

I realize not everyone wants to discuss their demise… Sorry, did we talk about this already? Anyway, to each his own. I'm saying I detest gossip. All it takes is for one person to see me coming out of Bennett's office and blam! Rumours and innuendo spread like wildfire, and suddenly, you're on the cover of People Magazine. Imagining I could be the subject of gossip sickens me. Then again, who can blame them? Dishing secrets is human nature, I suppose. I should resign myself to the fact that my disease will become the subject du jour at some point. Generally, people like to steer clear of mumbling, brain addled, demented folk, who shit themselves and sound like Kooky Cookie, in case it's catching. I know, I know, it's much more likely to be an emotional thing that keeps people away; like what do I do, what do I say? Let me help you; two words... I'm sorry, or, that sucks - that's the entire shebang.

Anyway, I've decided to keep this between us for now!

Who are you kidding? There won't be gossip because there's nobody to gossip about you.

Do you have to be cruel? What does that mean anyway? My family loves me. No matter what you do you asshole, you can never change that.

By the way, have I mentioned someone is stealing my clothes? Did I tell you that already? Sorry.

A non sequitur... again? Don't state the obvious!

They think I won't miss a scarf or two. Can't be Paige; she doesn't like my style. So, if it isn't her, it must be you know who; and now that she knows where my keys are, she's probably stolen my car and given it to her kooky mother.

I am not, paranoid!

SHE KILLED MY FLOWERS

"I'm on to you; I can't smell it through the window."

"I beg your pardon?"

"Don't play dumb with me, bitch. My flowers are all wilted!"

"How dare you? What does any of this have to do with me?"

"You don't think I know the brown patches in the grass are from poison dripping all over the yard?"

"What are you talking about? I never touched your flowers, or your grass. I've never even been in your yard."

"Liar! Where's the poison? Hand it over!"

"You're crazy. There's no poison! And maybe if you watered your flowers, they wouldn't be dead."

"So, you **are** spying on me?"

"You're ridiculous. Why would I do that?"

"How else would you know if I was home? I've seen you skulking. If you're trying to gaslight me, it won't work."

"You're nuts! I don't know what you're talking about."

"And you're full of shit!"

"All right... that's enough. Get away from my house and go back to the loony bin where you belong."

"And where are my cheques?"

"What cheques?"

"The ones you steal from my mailbox?"

"I don't even know which mailbox is yours. If you weren't nuts, you'd realize I need a key to get into it."

"And that's why you stole it, isn't it? Admit it!

"What? Now you're accusing me of stealing your mailbox key?"

"And my car keys. It was you who put them in the cupboard, wasn't it?"

"What?"

"You can't cash the cheques!"

"Well, if I can't cash them, why would I take them?"

"I... I... You're a bitch, that's why. You stole my keys, and now you're trying to kill me with poison. That's why I can't think - the poison's in my brain."

"I'm calling the police."

"Call them! I'll show them my flowers. They'll put you in jail."

"Oh, my word; what are you doing? Stop it! Stop it right now. **Don't you dare!**"

"Ma, you're in a lot of trouble. What were you trying to do?"

"She killed my flowers, David."

"I don't care. You can't pee in someone's yard."

"What? I did no such thing!"

"The police said you peed in her rose bushes."

"That's ridiculous! She's lying."

"Why would she do that? Ma, she's pressing charges. You could go to jail for up to sixty days, or pay a fine of five hundred dollars."

"They should put **her** in jail. Did you see my flowers? They're dead, all of them! And how do you explain the brown patches in the lawn?

"Grubs? We've got them too. Ma... what's gotten into you? I expect this kind of behaviour from some malicious punk."

"Don't lecture me. I'm still your mother."

"What do you expect me to say? I didn't know my mother was a criminal. What you did was... outrageous, and vulgar. Frankly, I'm shocked!"

"What was I supposed to do?"

"For starters, not pee in your neighbour's yard? You should apologize, Ma."

"I will not!"

"Fine."

"You don't believe me, do you, David? You think **I'm** crazy?"

"Ma, I don't know what to think. What reason would your neighbour have for poisoning your flowers? Did you have a disagreement? Argument? What?"

"She's psycho, that's what."

"Okay. Can you prove she poisoned your flowers?"

"AND grass!"

"… And grass?"

"No. How **can** I?"

"Where's your phone?"

"It's… uh… there, on the thingy."

"Look, this is a camera. I'll show you how it works."

"Oh, David. I can't…

"No, no, no. You don't even need to turn the phone on. You double-click this button on the side, and the camera comes on. See, easy. In the future, if you see her in the yard, take a picture, and I will deal with it. Okay? Ma?"

"Fine."

"And stay away from her, understand? I mean it. I'm going over to see if I can smooth things over, and get her to drop the charges."

"You seem to care more about her, than me."

"Don't be ridiculous. Do you want to pay five hundred bucks, or go to jail?"

"No."

"Okay, then. What would I tell, Raine? Hmm? Gramma is in jail for peeing in her neighbour's yard?"

Oh, damn. Damn! Damn! I hadn't considered that. Stupid! Stupid! Stupid!

"You're right, David. I'm sorry. I'm sorry. Please don't tell Raine."

"I don't plan to. I'm even too embarrassed to tell, Meg. Now, stay put, until I get back."

"David… Please don't be mad at me. I have a lot on my mind."

"You've lost your mind!"

"Don't say that! Please don't be angry with me."

"Fine, but I mean it, Ma, - no going over to her house, no yelling over the fence, no sending nasty notes, no anything. Right?"

"Yes. I'm sorry. I'm sorry, David."

"Stay put!"

DENIAL AIN'T A RIVER

"Hey, Meg… I've been wondering what to get, Ma for her birthday. Any thoughts?"

"How should I know, David?"

"Okay… not the response I was expecting. What's wrong?"

"You know what? Why don't you and Paige figure it out for a change? Why do you always leave everything up to me?"

"Whoa! I'm not **leaving** anything up to you, Meg, I'm asking your opinion. It's not as if I expect you to be the birthday whisperer and pull the perfect gift out of thin air."

"Fine. You want my opinion? Here it is. We agreed that Paige needed to check in with your Mum."

"Are you on this tangent again? Meg, for the last time, I can't **force** my sister to come home! She's a grown woman, not an employee I can boss around."

"Right... your sister. A sister who never sees her mother."

"And what do you want me to do Meg? You think I can wave a magic wand and poof; what's been broken between them, that's been twenty-five years in the making would suddenly heal? Whatever their issues, they can't be resolved overnight, and anyway, it's not my place to fix their crap. Shit, I'm barely holding my own. I can't do it.

"But, you expect me to, don't you?"

"What are you talking about? I haven't asked you to do a thing, and you couldn't if you tried."

"Seriously? Do you recall the conversation we had about me taking time for myself; about you pitching in? What happened to that? I'm still the chauffeur, maid, chief cook and bottle washer, **and** I haven't had a break from your mother. **Your** mother, David. **Your** mother! You **promised** me you would check in; do shopping, take her to the doctor... any of this ring a bell?"

"I'm sorry, Meg, things have been crazy at work."

"Yeah. Life is inconvenient."

"Come on, Meg, that's not fair."

"You're right… It's not fair. Not fair to me, your mother, and especially not fair to us. We're falling apart, David… If we don't get back on track… our marriage is dangerously close to falling apart."

"You can't be serious? Was that for dramatic effect?"

"David, I'm feeling overwhelmed, sad, unappreciated, and unloved."

"You're not the only one, Meg. The disconnect is there for me too, but I'm doing the best I can."

"Are you? Don't shake your head, it's a legitimate question."

"I can't talk about this anymore. Work is work; you're here, so…

"What? I'm here? Are you kidding me? Ha-ha-ha. Well, guess I'll get myself a full-time job, so I can go traipsing around the world, and neglect my responsibilities too. Do I need to remind you I put my career on hold so we could have a baby, make a home? And do you remember what happened next? That's right, my mom got sick, so I put my career on the back burner for another three years. And now that life is giving me the opportunity to get back on my feet, you want me to be your mother's nursemaid? I won't do it, David. I can't."

"And there it is... the truth. You're afraid. I get it."

"You don't get it. I'm not afraid for myself; I'm afraid for you. There's a long road ahead of you, David. Your mother is your responsibility - yours and Paige's, so you better figure it out, and fast."

"And I told you, Ma, doesn't need a nursemaid, and Paige is not neglecting her responsibilities, she's working. If Ma needed her, Paige would be here."

"My God, David, she does need her. And you want to talk about fear? Fine. From the moment I mentioned your mum might have dementia, you moved into full-fledged denial. You're defensive and combative."

"Look who's talking! And it's not denial when there's nothing to deny. You just can't admit your mother's illness gave you PTSD or something."

"Yes... those horrible years did leave scars on my psyche, but that's not what's going on here. I'm the only one who spends time with her; me and Raine. When's the last time you stopped in for a chat, or took her to the library, or for lunch? So, don't, David. Don't try to make this about my fears. This is about you, and your stubborn unwillingness to see what's right in front of your face. And why can't you speak to your sister?"

"Hey, Paige, it's me. Ma's going senile."

"Yes, David, that. She should also be apprised of the accident with the stove, the irritability. I don't understand why you can't you tell her?"

"Honestly? Because there's nothing to tell. I don't see the dementia boogie-man around every corner. I don't see losing things, or getting pissed as a sign that it's time to ring the fire bell at the psyche ward. God, Meg, I am so tired of this, and I'm sick to death of you being angry all the time."

"Well, maybe I wouldn't be angry if you'd open your eyes to what's going on. I'm exhausted, David, and you don't seem to care. And… I'm not mad… I'm sad… and lonely. Do you realize, we haven't spent more than an hour together when we weren't arguing? Do you remember the last time we were intimate, because I can't? You don't even kiss me anymore."

"That's not true."

"Really? The last time we had sex was months ago; our anniversary. But, fine, not another word, because contrary to what you believe, I'm sick to death of having this argument over and over too. I'm tired of you pretending everything is hunky dory. I'm tired, period. From now on, when you bury your head in the sand, I'll let you. Oh... one final thing. If you don't speak to Paige this week, I will."

"**All right, Meg!** I'll give Paige a call."

Gah! All I wanted was to get input on a birthday gift; not go another twelve rounds."

BROACH THE SUBJECT

"So, has the mystery of the missing keys be solved?"

"Yeah. That's why I'm calling. Raine found them in the cupboard, but listen, there're other things I need to talk to you about."

"The cupboard? Ha-ha-ha. Mother must be losing it."

"Don't say that, Paige!"

"Uh, that was a joke, D. Aren't you supposed to be the one with the sense of humour? What's wrong?"

"It's just... Meg's got it in her head, Ma has dementia or something. We've been fighting about it non-stop for months."

"Oh, no. I'm sorry. What's going on?"

"Weird stuff...

115

"What do you mean, weird stuff? Can you be a teensy more articulate?"

"I don't know, Paige. Meg says, Ma's acting weird."

"That's surprisingly unhelpful, David, and will you please stop saying, I don't know. **Has** Mother been acting, weird?' Come on, baby brother. Use your words."

"Christ, Paige, honestly? I'd say it's just Meg, being Meg. She still has nightmares after what she went through with her mom. She assumes I have dementia when I forget to put down the toilet seat. Shit."

"Okay. What are **your** thoughts?"

"Yeah, I mean… sometimes, Ma talks to herself, but so what, right? I talk to myself all the time."

"Is that it?"

"A while ago, Meg said, she got upset and yelled at her; told her to mind her own business. She even dropped the F-bomb."

"Ha-ha-ha. Okay. Any idea why?"

"Something about Meg plugging in her answering machine?"

"Okay, so far it doesn't sound like much."

"Exactly. That's what I said. Lost her car keys, had a little accident with the stove but...

"Wait. What? You didn't tell me about that. What happened?"

"She was cooking in her housecoat and her sleeve caught on fire. It wasn't serious; a couple of weeks and she was fine."

"You should have told me about that, David."

"I didn't think it was a big deal, Paige. If I called every time something stupid happened, we'd be on the phone all day."

"Going to the hospital is a pretty big deal, David."

"Please, don't get on me too. I can't handle two women chewing me out. Anyway, yeah... I should have called; sorry. Anyway, Ma's fine."

"Okay, anything else?"

"She could be depressed. She's been kinda gloomy lately."

"Can you broach the subject with her?"

"Cripes, is, 'broach,' the word of the month?"

"What?"

"Never mind."

"So, did you ask her if she's feeling low?"

"No, Paige, I didn't. You and Meg seem to think that conversation's an easy one, but I'm not good at that stuff."

"You just say…

"Hey, Ma are you depressed because you're losing your mind?"

"You're right. You are bad at it, ha-ha. There are more tactful ways of addressing the issue."

"I can't. Why do you think I'm calling you? Plus, I don't want Ma to feel...

"What, that you're concerned?"

"Have you met our Mother? Listen, Paige, is there a chance you can swing coming home? Meg and I are stressed to the max, and I'd like you to see Ma, face to face. Could you tell if she's got… dementia?"

"This isn't my field of expertise, David, and believe me, you'd notice if Mother were having issues before I would. I'm hardly around, but to answer your question, yes, I probably could."

"Yeah. Um, I don't want you to feel guilty, Sis, but Meg and I are struggling. She's talking about… a separation."

"What?"

"As I said, things are dicey on the home front."

"I'm so sorry, David. When's the last time I was home, anyway?"

"It's been about eight months."

"Has it really? Wow. Time flies."

"Can you call, or send Ma an e-mail or something? She's got a Facebook account."

"I can't be on social media, David, and even if I could, I don't have the time. Besides, the less Mother hears from me, the better. I'm sure you've noticed, we're not best buds. But, look, I get it. You and Meg always hold down the fort, so, uh… I'm leaving for Boston on Friday, and then I'm in Calgary for a workshop, but I promise to come home after that."

"Great! That syncs up perfectly with Ma's birthday."

"Oh, shit."

"You forgot?"

"I did, yeah, but that works out well. What's the plan?"

"We have a new restaurant in town called, Water's Edge. Guess where it is?"

"Uh… on the water?"

"You guessed! Ha-ha."

"She'll love it. Okay, sounds great. Make the reservations and text me the details. And, David?"

"Yeah?"

"Keep me posted in the meantime, huh?"

"I will."

"My love to Meg. And don't worry, I'll chat with her when I'm home. I'm sure everything will be fine."

"I hope so."

"Do some yoga or something, okay?"

"Ha-ha. Yeah. Bye."

LIFE SUCKS AND THEN YOU DIE

I hate birthdays. If anyone tells me, I'm only as old as I feel, I'll punch them right in the mouth! Brain fog, dry mouth, exhaustion and Arthur-Itis, so, yeah, ancient!

And what the hell is with our bodies eating us alive? One day, our immune systems decide hey, let's party? Cannibals! And yes, I said, Arthur-Itis. Corny, right? I told you… **old!**

If we're honest, cake and presents aren't the focus at our age. Birthdays are about being introspective; they're about zeroing in on the million things we didn't accomplish, and in my case, never will. So, what should I celebrate; a shrinking brain, a daughter who hates me, or a son who's so busy, the only time I see him is when I set myself on fire? Yay.

I remember once, seeing a boy torturing ants. He had the poor things under a magnifying glass, and was trying to set them on fire. I can relate! For the last few years, my brain's been scorched, pulverized, and my memories scattered by the winds of time and disease. So, whoopee, another trip around the sun.

Birthdays are like laser beams; pointed reminders the clock is ticking. Yay, again! I'm not sure being born is anything to celebrate anyway. Some days I wish I hadn't been. Yeah, yeah, it's a wonderful life - bullshit. I've made a mess of mine. One kid hates me, the other one doesn't care, and Howdy Doody just keeps smiling.

Time is slip, slip, slipping away, and the realization that life… my life is slipping with it… well, that's nothing to party about.

I live my entire existence in the past tense… did, was, used to, had. I experience nothing new. How can I? But, I smile and go through the motions, because if I don't, there'd be a barrage of questions, none of which I'm prepared to answer. So, if there's any merit in celebrating, it's for everyone else's benefit.

If a memory falls in the forest, will I remember?

Oh, and in case you're wondering? I kicked that kid's ass! Even ants deserve a life.

Why can't I just… die? I'm not being morose, just practical.

We're all dying.

I know, but I won't remember that I'm dying, will I? It's not fair!

Remember what we used to tell the kids? Life isn't fair?

Oh, shut up! Don't you dare throw my words back in my face!

All I'm saying is that if I had a choice between sleep-walking through overtime, or being present until sudden death, I'm choosing the firing squad!

Was, 'get your affairs in order,' number one, or two in that stupid brochure? Anyway, they're not the ones who won't remember the faces of their children, are they?

Here's another juicy question. Are any of my accomplishments even worth remembering, or is that too subjective a query? I'm no, Shakespeare or Jesus. Mother Teresa said, we can do no great things - only small things with great love. Well, I'm no saint either. I didn't strive for mediocrity, but in the grand scheme of things, that's what I'm leaving. There's no time left for greatness.

Time to give up. What else can I do against the Bearer of Obscurity? I know I'm disappearing, I can feel myself moving towards translucence. Translation? Invisible.

I tell ya, Cellophane, Mrs. Cellophane
Should have been my name, Mrs. Cellophane
'Cause you can look right through me
Walk right by me and never know I'm there

I had it comin'. I couldn't have said it better. How can I hope anyone will remember me, if I can't remember myself?

If you had a week to live, a month, or even a year, would that be a blessing? Time to tie up loose ends? Now, what if someone said, you'd live for years but as a mean, cranky, drooling, soiling mess? The only reason I try at all, is for Raine. I can't bear to disappoint her.

Okay, fine, you got me! I'm pitying myself; also, part of the birthday thing! You want me to be angry... lash out; cry? You relish the torture don't you, you spineless specter?

It's not your fault my trusty intellect. You didn't ask to be shrunken like one of the skulls in my creepy stories. It's that monster inside us; The Destroyer of Messages, the Nazi Experimenter, filling us with tangles and plaque; squashing every morsel of hope and kindness, before it bloats into oblivion.

There's nothing left for me except an agonizing descent into hell; and then what? Heaven?

Sylvia Browne used to say heaven's like earth, only better; greener greens, bluer blues - peaceful, filled with light. You remember her, she was a psychic that used to listen to dead people; had a spirit guide; sold thousands and thousands of books? Well, slick Sylvia was a charlatan and a liar. She sold false hope... if there is such a thing. Placebos are mighty powerful!

That's right. That's right! Listen up! There is no Black Menace- Om~ No inflammation Om~ A haven of peace and calm Om~ Two hemispheres working in harmony Om~ There are no lost connections Om~ Everything is firing on all cylinders Om~ Electricity flowing Om~ Memories restored Om ~

I watched a Ted Talk, where the guy said, biography is biology.

Are you telling me this is my fault? What on earth could I have done that allowed this monster into my head? Ah, yes, it must have been the time I was daydreaming about teeth noshing my brain. No? Okay then - what? Little heartaches? Did kid number one open a crack for the blackness? Oh... no, no, no... don't go there.

I don't buy it! Most of us don't live the life of Riley. Living is painful, but I've been lucky, my sorrow to joy ratio has been sixty-forty. That's not bad compared to some. However, according to Mr. Ted Talk, I've had a shitty biography! It could be true.

Have you been paying attention to the experts? One out of every two people will get cancer. That's fifty percent! Absurd! Diseases are making a come back too, because anti-vaxers have fewer brains than I do! Anyway, who am I to say whether our ordinary lives cause sickness? I'm no biologist.

*Then... I'm **not** responsible for this horror? Or I **am**? Ugh.*

I'm a firm believer in truth, painful or not; even though many truths can't be quantified. For instance, I **know** God's out there, somewhere. And don't be a dick and ask why he doesn't step in every time we fuck up. I can't answer that, and those claiming to have the answers, are full of shit. There **is** no reason for suffering, other than being trapped in these skin and bone life-boats. They get holes; we sink - that's it!

We should have spent more time contemplating heaven than trying to avoid hell.

Oh, Lord, please... I've been a good girl. Please grant me a miracle! Not for myself; for my kids. Ask anything of me, Lord. I'll do it!

Oh, stop it! No bargaining, remember?

*I **don't** remember... that's the point! Besides, I'm entitled to change my mind.*

Lord, please... send me a sign. Give me a miracle, I beg you! Mission work... soup kitchens, prisons. I'll do it. Please, just tell me what you want me to do!

What bothers me most is how my illness will affect Raine. How will she feel when Gramma can't recognize her anymore? I know Paige and David will carry on, but Raine - oh dear God, my sweet little Rainey.

No! No! **No! Damn it!** *You know the rule -* **No crying!**

A dear friend used to say, life sucks, and then you die. I'm not as cynical as all that, but it does sum it up rather succinctly.

So, another birthday… Guess I'll have to celebrate... for, Raine.

THE WATER'S COMING IN

"This is lovely, David. The view is gorgeous. My goodness, you can see clear across the lake; so calming."

"We knew you'd like it, Ma. We can all benefit from some calm, right, kiddo?"

"I'm calm, Daddy."

"You are?"

"Yup, but you and Mommy should watch the boats. You're stressed."

"You think so, huh?"

"Yup. My teacher says painting relieves stress."

"Ha-ha-ha. She does? In that case, we should all take up painting."

"I know I'd be less stressed if you put all your paints away when you were finished. How about that?"

"Mom! ...Auntie Paige, would you like to learn how to paint? I could teach you."

"I'd love that, Rainey, but I'm not very good at that sort of thing."

"That's okay. Gramma, would you paint with me?"

"I would honey, but it's hard for me to hold the brush. Gramma's got arthritis."

"I can help you hold the brush. Can I come over Monday after school?"

"I'm not sure. I think I'm at church that day."

"How about, Tuesday?"

"How about I call you when I have some free time, okay?"

"Okay. Auntie Paige? How long are you staying?"

"A little while, why?"

"Because silly. I want you to paint with me."

"I promise I'll find some time for that, okay?"

"Okay, but it has to be after school."

"Oh, David, this ambiance is enchanting. I read about how they pinched the Chef from a prestigious hotel in Italy. And the reviews? Fantastic; jammed every night! How did you manage to get reservations? I heard they're booked for months."

"Mother? Why do you assume David got the reservations?"

Here we go.

"You're absolutely right, Paige, I shouldn't assume. Did **you** make the reservations?"

"No, but I could have."

"Ugh. Paige… could we keep the animosity down to a dull roar this evening?"

"You're right, Mother… sorry."

"What's, an-i-mosity mean, Gramma?"

"It means something that happens between Auntie Paige, and me."

"Is it something nice?"

"Raine? Can you tell me what the letters spell on that big white boat?"

"M E M O R I E S - Memories?"

"Very good! That's the name of the boat."

And what's disappearing from my brain.

"I know."

"Okay, but did you know all boats have names, and they're usually girl's names?"

"Why?"

"Because long ago, sailors named their boats after goddesses. Now, boats have all kinds of names. Aren't they lovely just bobbing along in the water?"

"I've never been on a boat before, Gramma, have you?"

"Yes, but I'm not crazy about them. They are pretty to look at though."

"Why don't you like being in them, Gramma?"

"I'm not sure."

I remember something about water...

Slip… Slap…. Blap… Plop.

"Please don't leave me, Mummy!"

"You'll be fine. I'll come to get you when the party's over."

"I don't like it here. The water's coming in!"

"No, it isn't. Shhh. Listen…

"What?"

"It's music and laughing… from the house. Can you hear it?"

"Yes."

"I'll be that close, now, try to sleep."

"No, I can't. Mummy, I don't like it here. It's dark, and the water's gonna come in."

"Honey, this is a houseboat; it's designed to be on the lake. I know you can hear the water, but it's okay, it won't come in, I promise; and it isn't dark at all. The moon is shining right through the window.

"Mummy, the water's on the stairs."

"I know, it's okay. It won't get any higher than that."

"I'm gonna drown."

"Do you think I'd leave you here to drown, silly?"

"I don't want to stay here, please Mommy, I want to go to the big house."

"Just close your eyes. I'll be back soon! Nighty-night!"

"No, Mummy. No! I don't like it here. Please don't leave me. Mummy!"

"Shhh... close your eyes..."

"No, Mummy! Mummy! I'm scared! Please don't leave me! Mummy! Mummy!"

"Gramma? **Gramma**? Are you listening?"

"What? I'm sorry, I was daydreaming."

You are such a bastard! Can't you see I'm with my family? My granddaughter? It's my birthday dinner, for God's sake! You don't care about any of that, do you?

Oh, shut up! Stop talking to yourself. You sound like that repulsive creature from those Ring movies; My precious, my precioussssses.

I'm feeding you, aren't I? You thrive on nastiness. Or, are you feeding me? What if I called you by your real name… Alz… Alz… No! I can't!

Denial?

*I'm not in denial! It's not that I **can't** speak your horrid name, I just refuse to!*

But, we're together; sharing the same space.

What are you telling me? Are you saying I can't fight something I can't name? Is this a trick? If I give you a name, will you slow down and leave me alone? Fine. I'll call you… Al.

You already call me, Al, you stupid moron!

No, I don't! Do I? Stop it! I'm not a moron… I just forgot! No more name calling. Let's be acquaintances, room-mates. I won't hate you, if you don't hate me.

It's nothing personal, just my nature.

I have a nature too, Al, but you don't care about that, do you? Like the letters on the boat, you'll erase every memory one by one until they're all gone, won't you? You're nothing but a thief!

"All right, everyone ready to order?"

SURPRISE!

"What's the surprise, Mummy?"

"If I tell you, it won't be a surprise. Go get dressed. I laid your clothes out for you on the bed."

"This is my church dress."

"I know. It's okay. You can wear it just for today."

"Mummy? What time are we going to Giorgio's?"

"We're not going this year."

"We're not? Why? We always go for spaghetti today."

"I know, but this year we're doing something else; something special. It's a surprise, remember? Come to the backyard."

"Wow. Hats? Pretty tablecloths, and everything. It looks nice. Who are the hats for? Are they part of the surprise?"

"Part, but there's more."

"What is it? Tell me! Tell me!"

"All right. I thought this year, you could have a party."

"With you, and Baba and Dad?"

"Yes, and a few others."

"Is Auntie Helen coming?"

"No. Just me, Baba, and Baba and Dziadek."

"And Dad too?"

"I'm not sure about, Dad."

"Aww. He said he was coming."

"He still might. Guess who else?"

"Who? Who?"

"You sound like the pigeons. Guess you'll just have to wait and see."

Our neighbours to the back of us, keep like a million pigeons in a huge cage. They don't who-who, they coo-coo.

When I play outside, they get all excited and flap their wings like crazy. Their feathers fly out of the cage, and the wind blows them all over the place; even in our yard. Baba says the **neighbours** are cuckoo, cause the birds are dirty and make shit all over the grass. Mummy gets mad at her when she uses those kinds of words, but it makes me laugh!

I asked Baba what she thinks they keep pigeons for, and she said, "dey kill dem, an eet." Mummy got mad at her for saying that too!

We don't live on Northcliffe anymore; cause Mummy and Daddy got a divorce. Now we live with my other Baba.

I hate this house. Before we moved in, an old man lived here, and he smelled like pee! Bleh. Baba says he used his chair as a toilet and died in it too. We threw the chair out, and Baba cleaned the house until her fingers bled, but her fingers looked okay to me. Regardless, she says the smell is only in my head.

This house is teeny-tiny; it's called a bungalow. There're a lot of smelly cars and buses on our street, and I have to walk far to get to school; especially if I go around Brucie Feingold's house.

Last week, he hit me with a tree branch. He picks on other kids too. Once, I was late for school, because I had to wait for Brucie to leave first and he's **always** late. The principal sent a note saying I got a detention. I told Mummy it was because I woke up late that day. I didn't tell her about Brucie Feingold, 'cause she says I should fight my own battles.

It's my birthday today! I'm eight!

Mummy and I always go for spaghetti on my birthday; that's my favourite food in the whole wide world, but this year, she planned a surprise; a party with hats, balloons, and everything. I told her I don't like parties, and she got mad.

"I've gone to a lot of trouble young lady, so I expect you to be on your best behaviour. You're the hostess."

That means it's up to me to show everybody a good time.

"Why do I have to hostess? It's my birthday?"

"Stop pouting, or I'll give you something to pout about."

I hate it when she says that.

My stomach is full of butterflies 'cause I don't like surprises either. I wish we were going to Giorgio's.

"Your guests are arriving."

"Where? Where are they?"

138

"They're coming, they're just getting out of the car."

"Angela? Angela! Angela! Mummy, it's Angela... and Theresa, and... Rimmy, and Sergio! Oh my gosh, it's all my friends from Northcliffe."

"Feeling better now?"

"This is the best birthday ever! Is Daddy here?"

"Not yet. All right, greet your guests, and take them to the backyard."

"Hi everybody. Wanna play?"

"Do you have to pee?"

"Mum! Whisper!"

"Well, do you? Now's the time, before you start playing."

"Okay, but I don't."

"Are you sure?"

"I'm sure."

"It looks like you're holding it in."

"Mum! I'll go in a second."

"You're it! Ha-ha - tagged you - you're it!"

"Angela, Angela, let's be a team, we'll get Theresa and Rimmy. Sergio… you be home, okay?"

"Mummy, are you making hot dogs?"

"Yup."

"Did you buy chips?"

"Yup. And pizza's coming too. Stop running around and hit the can."

"I **will**, Mum! In a second! Where's Dad?"

"Stop worrying about dad, and more about peeing your pants!"

"Okay… You're it…. Ha-ha-ha."

"Pizza's on the way, guys."

"K, Mom!"

"I want you to go pee before the food gets here!"

"I wanna wait for Dad."

"Don't make me tell you again."

"There he is! Daddy! Daddy!"

Oh-oh.

SAVOUR THE SUNSET MY ASS

"Before we have cake, we brought some gifts for you to open, Ma. Here's present number one from, Meg and me."

"Mother, what's wrong? Your face is flushed."

"Nothing. It's from the wine, Paige, but thanks for bringing it to everyone's attention."

Oh God, I didn't! I couldn't have. Mom kept telling me to go. Oh, God! What do I do?

"Play nice you two!"

"Oh… lovely…. Thank you."

"Ma, you hardly looked. Are you okay?"

"Yes, fine… I saw what it was… a gift certificate for a mani-pedi."

142

"I thought we could go together. Mum? Mum?"

"Yes… that would be nice, Meg. Thanks."

"Are you sure you're all right, Mother?"

"It's just a headache. Would anyone mind, if I opened the rest of these at home?"

"But we haven't even had cake yet, Gramma! Please open your presents here! Please? Please? I picked this one out all by myself."

Don't cry! **Don't cry!** *It won't do you any good now, and you'll upset Raine!*

"You did? Then I love it already. All right, sweetheart, do you want to save the bow?"

"Uh-huh. Gramma, your hands are trembly."

"Well, I'm very excited. It's not every day I get a present from my favourite granddaughter."

"Tee-hee… you're silly, Gramma.   I'm your only granddaughter."

"You're still my favourite… What's this? Oh, Rainey, what a beautiful shawl, and my favourite colour too. Thank you, my sweet, sweet girl."

"It'll be nice for Fall, Ma; you can throw it over your shoulders, or over your coat?"

"Thank you… I love it."

"Gramma, why are you crying?"

"Sometimes when your heart is full, love overflows through your eyes. Come here so I can give you a big giganticus hug."

"Hee-hee. Gramma, you're squishing me."

"Mwah, mwah, mwah."

"Mother, this one's from me."

"Okay. Let's have a look! **Grey is the New Blond?** Savour the Sunset? What's this?"

"My new book; from my workshop series, called, The Wisdom Years. It's all about what people your age are doing these days."

"You mean, **old** people?"

"No, Mother; that's the point. Age is just a number!"

"Uh-huh. Tell that to my knees."

"I realize that for your age group - I call you, Generation Wise; mobility can be an issue, but you can do plenty of things that require little physicality. The book might inspire you to try something new. You don't want to hang around the house all the time, do you?"

"I am NOT housebound, Paige, and for your information, I do plenty."

"Such as?"

"I go to church, sing, read, visit friends."

"That's great, but hardly new! I was thinking more along the lines of public speaking, ballroom dancing, taking a cooking class, volunteering at a school, or perhaps reading stories at the library?"

"Ha-ha-ha; public speaking? Dancing? Oh, Paige, you can't be serious?"

"All right, but you could read to kids. You'd be great!"

Oh, wouldn't that be lovely; "and the big bad wolf said, I peed myself." Sorry kids, Gramma's got, Al!

"You hate it."

"No, I don't, Paige."

"You do. You're making that sour face! Well, it can't be exchanged, for obvious reasons, but I can get you something else."

"Oh, Paige, stop being dramatic! The book looks wonderful! Besides, how do I know if I like it or not? I haven't read it. And I **will**! I promise! Who knows; I might surprise you, and take up interior design or something. Thank you, dear! I mean it! It's amazing. Congratulations."

"Thanks, Mother... Oh, here's the cake! Happy Birthday to you. Happy Birthday to you. Happy Birthday dear Gramma, Happy Birthday to you!"

"Make a wish, and blow out the candles, Gramma!"

"You help me, okay, Rainey? Ready? One, two, three... Fooooo!"

"Yay!"

"What did you wish for, Gramma?"

I wish to remember this moment for the rest of my life; to brand all your faces into something that can't be forgotten. I long to have more time; before my memories are jigsaw pieces, and I become Humpty-Dumpty.

"You know the rule, I can't tell, otherwise, the wish won't come true."

"Thank you, everyone. I've had a lovely birthday, but between the wine and the coffee, I'm not sure whether I'll be up all night, or sleeping in the car on the way home!

"It's only once a year, Mother."

Yes, once a year. She doesn't understand; how can she? By next year, these faces...

"Ma? Is everything okay?"

"Why does everyone keep asking me? Once and for all, I'm fine! Will you all just leave me alone!"

"Don't be mad on your birthday, Gramma."

Oh, dammit. Don't spoil this moment for Raine! Don't you dare! It's not her fault you peed yourself like a fucking infant. Hold it together half-wit.

"Oh, sweetheart. I'm not mad; I'm only a little tired. Sorry. David, I'd like to go home; my headache's getting worse."

"Okay, Ma. I'll find the maitre d and settle up."

"Thank you, David. The rest of you should go ahead. I'd like to 'savour the sunset,' for a moment, like it says in the first chapter of Paige's book. See, I'm enjoying it already."

"Sarcasm, Mother?"

"Paige? Why can't you accept a compliment? I'm looking forward to reading this... and I'm... proud of you."

"Thank you, Mother."

"Okay... off you go. I need to visit the Ladies' Room. I'll be out shortly."

"Fine. We'll wait outside. Don't be long!"

"I wasn't planning on dawdling."

Where are cloth napkins when you need them? Just stuff it down... no one will notice.

Oh, God. I hate you... you... bastard!

TICK,TICK,TICK,TICK,TICK

What say you?

Guilty!

Let me tell you what it's like to be on death row. First comes denial, then pleading and crying, followed by bargaining, sadness, and acceptance, but not necessarily in that order.

Like a defective seventy-eight, emotions play over, and over, and over. Blip... blip... blip; spinning in the old noggin, like that ride where the floor drops out beneath you, and the only things holding you up, are inertia and centrifugal force?

Asphyxiated by fear, adrenaline courses up and down your arms like Bernstein conducting the Philharmonic. Your knees buckle, your mouth tastes like sand; your heart pounds like a time bomb; tick,tick,tick,tick,tick,tick,tick.

You wait for the explosion, but it never comes; it just keeps, tick,tick,tick,tick,ticking. Your head rings with the commotion of a thousand chimes clanging in such a cacophony, you don't hear yourself scream...

I'm innocent!

But, it doesn't matter, because there's no chance for appeal, no parole; no mercy. Al is judge and jury. It's decided. From here on in, you're under house arrest with a killer that puts Jack the Ripper to shame.

There's no relief; no firing squad, no lethal injection; just drooling, shitting and death.

Make no mistake; he **will** kill you, but not before the slow, day by day... hour by hour... minute by minute, tick,tick,tick,tick,ticking, torture.

I am alive by inertia. Perhaps we all are. The heart continues to lub-dupe, lub-dupe, lub-dupe, even while the brain shrinks, shrinks, shrinks. Maybe that's why some of us are couch potatoes, while others can't sit still for a second?

My mother-in-law, God rest her soul, had one part of her body in motion at all times; a swinging foot; back and forth, back and forth, back and forth; twiddling thumbs, tongue clicking... incessant humming. After spending an hour with her, I needed a nap; and I'd done nothing all day but sit on my ass. That's an illness too - interminable movement Perhaps an addiction to needing to feel alive? I understand. Sometimes I stick a pin in myself to make sure I'm still here.

Will they guess my sickness, or will I have to lay prostrate and spill my guts and confess? I... I... I have, Al. Dun, dun, dun!

"He tied me to the railroad tracks." Where's Underdog, when I need him?

Or, will I look at them one day; eyes vacant, brain atrophied, and say, I'm sorry my dears, I don't have a fucking clue who you are. That's providing my words haven't turned to dust and blown out my ass by then.

All dignity... gone. A slow life leak, like the puddle I left at the restaurant.

"Th-Th-The, Th-Th-The, Th-Th... That's all, folks!"

Or like the dead in T. S. Eliot's, The Hollow Men...

"This is the way the world ends. Not with a bang, but a whimper."

Lovely.

KENSINGTON

Pawich's Meat Market is covered in sawdust. Baba says it's there to keep the floor from being slippery. A man with hairy ears and big yellow teeth... *The better to eat you with, my dear,* overhears our conversation and tells me the sawdust is there to clean up the blood. He sniggers as he swallows my shoulder with his giant, sweaty hand. I tear away and hide behind Babcha, who gives him a scowl.

The butcher counter runs the length of the store, and is stuffed with blocks of jellied meat, chicken legs, ham, bologna, dead rabbits, liver and other yucky stuff. Yech! I hate liver. One time, Mummy forced me to eat it, and I threw up.

Blood pools along the glass, soaking the string that keep big blobs of meat from falling apart. Maybe the crooked-toothed man was right?

"Numer trzy?"

We're early, and we're still not number one? Ugh. Everybody has to take a numbered piece of paper from this red machine, and then you have to wait until your number's called. Sometimes the machine breaks and then you have to wait even longer.

The sun pours through the big glass window at the front. Baba says we come early, so we don't get baked alive, but I'm hot already.

There's the roly-poly man again, winking at me. His yellow teeth turn orange in the sun. I tell Baba, and she says that's why it's important to brush, so my teeth aren't yucky.

"Cztery?"

Only four?

"Baba? … Baba?"

"Co?"

"What number are we? Are we number five?"

"Nie. Jesteśmy numerem osiem."

"Eight? That's too long! Do we have to stay?"

Three people stepped on my foot, and one lady whacked me in the ear with her stupid purse!

153

"I wanna go! Can I sit in the car? Please? Baba? Owww! You're squishing me. I wanna go, Baba. Can I go?"

"Bądź cicho!"

"I don't want to be quiet. I wanna go! It's hot! Pleeeeze, can I wait in the car?"

"Jest goręcej w samochodzie."

"No, it isn't. The car's not hot."

"Idź tam i policz słoiki."

"I don't want to count jars. Where?"

"Tam na półce."

"This shelf? Okay, but I only know my numbers to ten."

One... two... three... green stuff... one, two, three, six, red peppers. Too many jars of borscht to count.

"Baba, can we buy borscht? Baba... Baba... Baba!"

"Co?"

"Can we buy borscht?"

"Nie, tworzę własne."

"But why do you have to make it, when you can buy it already made?"

"Baba? Mummy taught me how to count in seconds, wanna hear? Baba? Baba? Wanna hear? Baba?"

"Tak. Dobrze, powiedz mi."

"One, Mississippi, two Mississippi, three Mississippi, four Mississippi...

"To jest bardzo dobre."

"Thank you. Can we go now? **I wanna go!**"

"Bądź cicho!"

"I don't want to be quiet. One day, I'll yell so loud, I'll make the house fall down!"

"Musisz być cierpliwy."

"Does being patient mean I have to wait?"

"Tak!"

"Then, I don't want patience. ...Baba, the Kobassa is wet. Why is it wet? **Baba... why is it wet?**"

"Oy... Co?"

"Why is the Kobassa wet?"

"Nie jest mokra, pocenie się."

"Sweating?"

"Tak."

"Yeah, it's hot. I'm sweating too!"

"Numer sidem?"

"Tutaj!"

"Babcha, are we next? Is it our turn? Are we next?"

"Osiem?"

"Tutaj."

Hey, pickles!

I escape from under boobs and run towards the barrel in the corner. My fingers trace the icy copper bands. As I skip around the cask, faster and faster; the wooden planks spin like the frames in a movie.

Sometimes, Mummy sets up the projector downstairs, and we watch films of Baba picking a cemetery plot; that's where you go when you're dead. Afterwards, we had a big party, and everybody came; even Auntie Sophie, and Auntie Mary and Uncle Bob.

"Owww!"

Oh-oh. Stupid slippery sawdust! Baba's gonna be mad at me for fooling around. I better not say anything.

"Baba, are you finished?"

"Tak. Co się stało? Dlaczego krwawisz?

"I'm bleeding? I dunno!"

"Chcesz pikle?"

"Yes! Yes! Pickle! Pickle!"

A big pot-bellied man comes from behind the counter and removes the top of the barrel. I think you have to be fat to work here, 'cause the ladies' chi-chi's are popping out of their dresses, and their stomachs go, bloop, bloop, bloop in rolls down the fronts of their dresses.

The blood from my chin gets all over the man's apron, as he leans over, but it's okay, cause it's already bloody. I hope it's not liver blood.

I slip my hand under the dill that saturates the zesty brine, and pull out the biggest pickle I've ever seen. Mm-

mm. Saliva explodes in my mouth; pickle juice runs down my stinging chin. I don't care… Ooh, so sour.

"You all da time making mess wit peekle! Oy!"

Dziadek stays in the big turquoise car, because it's hard to find a good parking space. He gets mad when Baba lets me bring pickles in the car, 'cause sometimes the juice drips on the seat and makes it sticky.

Baba told me I have to be extra good today, cause Dziadek drank too much at the Legion last night, and has a hangover. I think that means his head hurts.

"Hi, Dziadek."

"Dlaczego co tydzień dajesz jej pieprzoną marynatę? Ona robi wielki bałagan!"

"Okay! I'll be careful not to drip."

"Be kviet, old man!"

"Na, Kleenex!"

Baba winks at me from the front seat.

"Why are we stopping at the drug store, Baba?"

"Żeby dostać Alka Seltzer za ból głowy dziadka."

"I thought, Alka Seltzer, was for your stomach?"

"Dziadek, is it good for your head too... Dziadek?"

"Cicho!"

"Okay, sorry. I'll whisper... Oh... here comes Baba with your medicine. You'll feel better now."

Plop, plop, fizz, fizz. Gulp, gulp, gulp.

"Baba! Something's wrong with Dziadek. He's choking! He's choking! There's foam coming out of his mouth. Wahhhhh.... wahhh."

"Oy, oy, oy... O Boże! Give pop wit Alka Seltzer, because no have wader at Droog Shtore. No cry. No cry. Dziadek, okay. Everybody okay. No cry now. Okay.... Okay."

"No... he's not okay. He's not breathing!"

"Arrgh! Próbujesz mnie zabić, kobieto?"

"Baba, did you try to kill, Dziadek?"

"No, no... I no keel. Ha-ha-ha. Next time, no pop. Ha-ha-ha. Okay, we go. Ha-ha."

"Dziadek... are you, all right?"

"Tak, tak. I okay. I okay. Cough! Oy! Cough!"

I can't wait to tell Mummy what happened. At first, it was scary, but then Baba and I laughed so hard, we almost peed our pants.

Dziadek looked like a big soda machine. Hee-hee.

Oh boy, we're here… Kensington Market bakery! When we bring goodies home, Mummy says the kitchen smells like heaven.

I like their rye bread; it's yummy with borscht. Baba, chews it with her gums. One time, I put her teeth in my mouth, and we laughed so hard, we both fell down.

Yum, yum… blueberry buns, with sugar on top. Babcha buys them every week. You have to get a number and wait in line here too, but it's fun, because you get to look at cookies and candies and cakes. Oh… marzipan!

"Baba, can I have marzipan? … Baba? Baba, where are you?"

"Baba?"

"B A B A!"

"Baba, where are you? I'm lost!"

STOP THE CAR

"Hi... I'm Betty. Please, come in. Your mom's in the kitchen."

"Oh, thank goodness, David! I was driving and missed my turn and I...

"It's all right, Ma. It's all right. Are you okay?"

"Yes... yes, I'm fine."

"Ma, please get in the car; I'll be there in a minute."

"But what about **my** car, it's...

"We'll get it later, Ma. It's okay. Go ahead. I'll be right there."

"Mrs.?"

"Oh, call me, Betty, please."

"Thank you. Uh, Betty… can you tell me what happened?"

"Well, I came out this morning to get my mail, and your mom was sitting on the stoop, crying. She was confused, and kept saying, baba, baba, over and over."

"That means grandmother in Polish and Ukrainian."

"Oh, I see. Well… Bill, my husband, asked your mom how she got here, and she mumbled something about a car. We asked the make and model, but all she could say, was that it was blue. There are several blue vehicles, but she wasn't able to identify which car was hers.

She couldn't tell us her name or address either. We were going to call the police, but she got frantic at the suggestion, so we checked her purse, and found her driver's licence. That's how we got her name. We would have taken her home, but she was so disoriented, we were afraid to leave her alone.

She insisted we call her daughter, and when we spoke to her, she gave us your number."

"My sister is so busy, I'm surprised you reached her, but, that's great. Thank you so much for taking care of my mother. I really appreciate it."

"Oh, no problem. I hope she's okay… It's none of my business, but has this happened before?"

"No, this is a first."

"It's scary getting lost. I've done it twice... but… I think what happened to your mom was more than an erroneous detour. As I say, she was quite upset.

"Can I give you something for your trouble?"

"Oh, no, no, absolutely not! If this ever happens to me, I hope someone would be kind enough to help me out."

"Well, we should be on our way. Thanks again for your kindness, Betty."

"Uh… David? I think your mom should go to the hospital. Could be a little stroke or something?"

"Good advice. I'll see how she's doing. Betty, I very much appreciate your kindness. Thanks again. Goodbye."

"Good Luck!"

"Ma, what happened?"

"I don't know."

"Are you, okay? I mean do you feel sick or anything?"

"No, just humiliated and stupid."

"Anyone can get lost, Ma, and you're not stupid. What were you doing in this part of town, anyhow?"

"Uh... I... uh...

"Were you coming to visit somebody, or picking something up for the bazaar?"

"I don't know, David, and I don't want to talk about it."

"All right. We can talk about it later. We'll pick your car up later, okay?"

"I don't give a damn about the car. Just take me home!"

"We can't just leave it there, Ma."

"I said, I don't care! I hate that street. Pick it up, tow it, fuck it. **I don't care!**"

"All right, Ma. Calm down."

"**Don't tell me to calm down, dammit**, and stop looking at me like I've got two heads. Last time I checked, getting lost wasn't a crime!"

"No... I'm just trying to understand what happened, that's all."

"There's nothing to understand. I got distracted and got out at the wrong exit. Now, please take me home, I've got a splitting headache."

"You've had a lot of headaches lately. Have you spoken to the doctor?"

"The headaches are because I'm always being interrogated, as if I'm a suspect in a murder investigation."

"That's not true, Ma. You've just been out of sorts lately."

"Well, I apologize for not acting in accordance with David's rules of behaviour!"

"Ma, please... Can't we talk about this calmly?"

"What's there to talk about? I got lost. The end."

"Well, is your GPS working?"

"David, for the love of God...

"Ma, we bought you the GPS so this kind of thing wouldn't happen. If it's not working, I'd like to know."

"That's probably how I missed the damn exit, checking the stupid GPS. It was recalculating, and there were so many cars behind me, I got nervous. I didn't want to stop and wait for it to correct itself, so I started driving, and then I didn't know where I was."

"Okay... that makes sense."

"Oh, well thank you."

"And why on earth would you call, Paige instead of me? She's out of town, remember?"

"I've already bothered you enough, I didn't want to tear you away from work again."

"Well, did you think she'd fly all the way from Kelowna to get you?"

"Do you expect me to remember everyone's schedule? Stop interrogating me."

"Ma, Betty said you couldn't tell her your name or address. That's a little concerning."

"Who the hell is Betty?"

"The lady whose house we just left?"

"Well, pardon me, but **I was upset!**"

"Ma, we should go to the hospital."

"No! Absolutely not! I've been to enough hospitals!"

"Ma… you may have had a stroke or something."

"I don't care. I'm not going! You should be at work. I don't want you to get into trouble."

"For heaven's sake, Ma, let me worry about work, okay? They won't care that I missed a morning."

"Well, I care! I am not going to the hospital. That's final. If you won't take me home, I'll get there on my own. Stop the car, RIGHT NOW! I want out!"

"Don't be ridiculous. I am not stopping the car."

"Then, take me home."

"All right, Ma… okay. I'll take you home. But, we will talk about this later."

"I… got lost - that's all… a little lost."

If only he…

And when will you tell him?

Shut up. You don't need to chastise me too! Stop talking!

AND WHAT IF IT'S ALZHEIMER'S?

"You should have taken her, David."

"I tried, Meg. What was I supposed to do, tie her to the back of the car and drag her to the hospital?

"If need be!"

"Don't be ridiculous, Meg. I can't kidnap her. Even if I'd taken her, how would I get her out of the car once we got there? What do you want from me? She didn't want to go!"

"Of course, she didn't **want** to go, David. She was scared and confused."

"By the time I got in the car, she was fine... completely coherent, and adamant about going home.

"I don't think I told you this, Meg, but the first week I got my licence, something like this happened to me too! I missed my exit and ended up in some bloody new subdivision with no street signs. It was totally off the grid. I circled around for hours before finding my way back to the main road. It rattled me!"

"Did you also forget your name, the make and model of your car, or end up crying on a stranger's stoop?"

"No, but I've forgotten my phone number before. All I'm saying, is that sometimes you have a brain glitch. She was humiliated, Meg. In that moment anyone could forget their address."

"David, has it occurred to you, this isn't the first time something like this has happened to your Mum? Remember how secretive my mother was? And what about the key incident? You're trying to protect her, but you're making things worse."

"Meg, can we please not have this argument for the umpteenth time? **My** mother is not **your** mother. If you'd stop comparing the two for five fucking seconds, you'd realize you're **looking** for something to be there that isn't. The key "incident" as you call it was last year, and nothing has happened since that would remotely suggest, Ma has dementia."

"Or, was losing her keys the only incident we're aware of?"

"Ugh."

"Why are you refusing to acknowledge what's right under your nose? Your mother needs to see a doctor, David, and she needs to be convinced to do so. It may not be dementia. What if Betty is right, and your mum's having issues with her heart; or it was a stroke? What happens the next time she's driving and has an episode, and kills herself, or God forbid, somebody else? Can you at least consider **that** possibility? What if she killed someone... a child perhaps... like Raine? Could you live with yourself?"

"David... we need to understand what's happening, for her sake. If your mum refuses, maybe you have to take matters into your own hands?"

"What? Go, behind her back? I don't know about that. Anyway, Paige is coming in this weekend. I'll talk to her."

"Oh, don't forget we're picking up Ma's car tonight. I'll call you when I'm leaving work, and you guys can meet me there. Shit... I really don't need this."

"I'm sorry, David. I know this is stressful. It's difficult for all of us, but the sooner we figure it out, the better."

"And... what if it is... Alzheimer's?"

"We'll cross that bridge when we get to it."

THE LOST DECADE

Do you recall coming back to life after you've had the flu? You dust the house, wash the car, cut the grass, then relapse for another week? Well, this is nothing like that! Functioning with, Al is like living the life of Benjamin Button, only my brain is moving to the back of the bus, while the rest of me is jet streaming, and screaming, towards decay.

Ooh, clever… wouldn't you say, Al?

I have a good sense of humour, and so far, Al hasn't gobbled it up. Humour must be the second course. The key to telling a good joke is a choice delivery, **and** excellent timing. Gotta have sizzle! David got my sense of humour; dry, witty, not shtick, you know?

Anyway, I die-gress. Die? … gress. Not funny? Well, they can't all be winners! Even the best comedians bomb.

Wait... is, Al like the flu, or not like the flu? What I'm trying to say is that this is not your garden variety back to bed for a few days, type of relapse. It's a relapse, followed by a pre-lapse. Sorry, I even confused myself on that one.

What the hell am I talking about? **Shut-up, Al!** *You're confusing me!*

Okay, let's skip the flu analogy. New topic.

As you may have noticed, my sizzle is waning to a fizzle. Al's playing chess inside my head, and I'm the Queen, King, Rook, and pawn.

Nope! No pawn jokes!

This reminds me of a joke my husband used to tell... Oh, wow! I haven't thought about, Baby Daddy, in ages. A.K.A. the worst joke teller of all time! When he opened his mouth at a party, guests would scatter like dish soap in grease. Or is it grease in dish soap? Whatever it is, I forgave him his punch-line debacles, as he did other things quite well. For instance, Baby Daddy could build a house out of nothing but wind and sand.

He's been dead, a long time. Twenty? Thirty years?

Damn, Al! Slow down! Give me a chance to catch my breath! I'm trying to figure something out here.

It was a sunny day; hot as blazes, not a cloud in the sky. Or, was it overcast? No, no, it was a sunny Sunday afternoon. I remember because I played hooky from church that day. Regardless, it was a scorcher; unusual for March... or was it, April? Whatever month it was, it was freaky hot, and Baby Daddy was out back doing whatever men do in sheds; putter, fiddle; read car magazines... other things – ahem! And you know that internal clock that tells us we've waited longer than feels comfortable, whether for a person, or a bus? Or, we check the cake right before the timer goes off?

Anyway, I was inside, seething with frustration because I'd asked him to do something important, and here he was wasting time.

To cool the tongue-lashing, he was about to get; I decided to bring him a cold beer. That's when I found him... lying in a heap; crumpled up like a pile of snotty tissues.

I went numb. My brain tried to process what I was seeing, but suddenly the world was moving in slow motion, and I couldn't think.

Baby Daddy had fallen on some pitchfork thingy, which jammed on his stupid mother's old couch. God, if I asked him to get rid of that thing once, I'd asked him a hundred times. One of the prongs was poking through the gash in his shin, and flies were already congregating over the pooling blood.

I started getting cranked up, as if my brain was suddenly propelled through a supersonic tunnel into real time.

"Idiot! What the hell are you thinking working on a blistering hot day like this? Have you lost your fucking mind?"

I went crazy. I knew he was dead, but there I was, cursing and screeching; trying to drag him out of that crematorium of a shed. I pulled, pushed, twisted, rolled him over; yanked him by the arms, the legs, and anything else I could grab, but he wouldn't budge. And, all the while I spewed obscenities over his corpse as if I was playing a part in some perverse comedy.

"How dare you die, you stupid son of a bitch! Look at this mess! Fuck!"

I was slipping and sliding in blood, soaked to the skin with sweat; dizzy from exertion and heat, and about a minute from losing consciousness. It was like a scene from Psycho, except I was doing all the screaming.

I don't remember calling 911, or seeing the ambulance arrive. They didn't even try to resuscitate him. The doctor said, it was a, myocardial infarction.

"I'm sorry…there's nothing I can do."

"A what?"

He could have said, heart attack, but, I guess, myocardial infarction sounded more official. Funny, the things we remember.

That's when I cried.

He was Sixty-four. No… **forty-six**… the prime of life, Baby.

Out poured the platitudes; too young, God must need another angel; on and on. Thanks. I feel a lot better now.

The dead don't require consolation, the living do. Ugh. Anyway, as my grandmother used to say, "when it's you time, it's you time!"

I could have done without this one, Al!

To be honest, I remember little else about my husband; the colour of his eyes, whether his hair was thick or thin? Hell, he could have been bald, or had tresses like Victor Mature. The only think I remember, is that he loved me. Isn't that enough? Don't misunderstand. Being married to Baby Daddy wasn't all roses and fairy-tales; but we had some great moments. Hey… some days you're the princess; other days you're the frog!

I refer to this decade as, The Hurry-Up, years. Hurry-up, we're late for dance; hurry-up, we're late for soccer. Hurry, hurry, hurry!

Step right up; see the woman with the shrinking brain!

Maybe these years are a blur because I wasn't able to slow down long enough to form any memories? Who knows?

Oh, it was jam-packed and full of... things... but the details? All muddled... The rest? Gone... like in, The Lost Weekend with Ray Milland. Only, this was a decade, and I wasn't drinking. At least, I don't remember drinking, although that might explain the lapses in memory.

The lonely, lost decade...

Now it's just me and you, Al.

That is **not** *funny!*

WHERE THE HELL'S THE SILVER LINING?

So, Paige came home, because David told her I got lost! Now, I wait for the onslaught of, what, where, when, why, and who? Ugh! They won't get answers because I can't remember what happened.

Losing oneself can be a physical, metaphorical, even an existential dilemma. Physically, I don't remember being lost, so I can't speak to that. Metaphorically... well, when the brain shrinks, the Id and Ego shrivel too; that's a good thing. This leaves existential disappearing. Hmm. To struggle with one's identity in the face of mortality? How can one not? Did I make sense?

My kids are beginning to suspect I'm ill, but they won't come right out and say I'm losing my mind, and I'm not sharing, diddly-squat.

One, of the reasons I'm not prepared to lose myself should be obvious; yes, the dying thing, but the other reason is, I'm just beginning to find myself.

I always imagined when it was time to die, I'd feel... fulfilled, sufficient; not give a shit about other people's opinions. I was so close to stepping outside mainstream and not giving a damn, I could taste it. But, I didn't make it; at least not on my terms. Oh, sure, soon enough I won't remember anyone's opinion, but it isn't a natural birth; it's being artificially induced. Al is not pro-choice.

Am I the only one who feels unfinished or inadequate? What does it matter? As we used to say, no sense crying over spilled... something... or is it... too late to shut the barn door once the cows escape?

Hold on... I just remembered something about leaving my car... somewhere... I did get lost, but at the grocery, right? What do you expect? Jacques Cartier couldn't find his way around in there. How many fucking aisles are there anyway? I used to be in and out of the grocery in under fifteen minutes; now I'm lucky if I'm out in under an hour!

Who designs these places anyway, The Museum of everything you ever wanted in one place? They force you to walk to the farthest corner for milk, and to the entire opposite corner for fruits and veggies, with the crap aisles sandwiched in between. And should there be entrances and exists at both ends? Last week, I sauntered into the mall, shopping cart and all, and wandered around for hours. Ugh.

They must design Megastores for those people who feel life isn't worth living unless they get in their ten thousand steps. Isn't shopping hard enough without walking a half marathon? Load the cart, unload the cart, load the cart, unload the cart. Fuck! Picking food from a field would be quicker.

And the grocery is... it's... I turn left on...

Give it up! You can't remember shit anymore!

That's not true! I just can't remember if I turn on the first street at the corner? It's called... um... sigh... FINE! Fuck you, Al!

Thank goodness I don't shop often; it's exhausting, so many aisles, so much food; not to mention it's like walking a half marathon. Ugh!

What? Did I repeat myself? Did I? Damn it! Was that a non sequitur? What the hell was I talking about?

So, Paige is home. Now, I'll be forced to listen to a diatribe from the three amigos of why it's a good idea for me to see the doctor. But, my darlings, I've already been, haven't I?

"Your brain's all tangled up, Mrs. Blah. You have mixed, wah-wah-wah-wah, with vascular dementia and Alz…"

Oh, very tricky; you almost got me to say it, didn't you, Dr. Blah-Blah? Oh, Al, you can eat me alive, but I'll never utter your filthy name. You disgust me!

"Blah, blah, blah with possibly good years in between."

Possibly? Know what I heard? Blah, blah, bah, you're fucked!

"Yes, I'll talk to my family the second I get home!"

"I'd rather pluck out my eyeball with a fork."

"Questions, Mrs. Blah?"

"I'd like a second opinion, and a third and forth."

What about ants, Dr. Blah? It's worth a try, isn't it? With their proficient work ethic, couldn't they peel away the goo; untangle the tangles?

I would be happier if they told me he who must not be named was coming after me. At least the no-nosed wizard doesn't steal your mind or keep you on such a tight leash your brain explodes. He doesn't stuff your head with brain-clogging poison; implant some twisted, demented disease that eats you alive. No, he just kills you. One minute you're alive, the next - poof, you're dead!

That's *how you do it, Al! You're nothing but a sadistic serial killer!*

We all have to die of something; it's just I want to remember that last something. I want to share meaningful, last words; have a warm smile for my kids; savour a fleeting notion about the world before I cross the river Styx. I envisioned imparting words of wisdom to my beautiful grandchild; telling her I love her; letting her know that even though she won't see me, I'll always be with her.

I know it's romanticized, so what? We want life to be a fairy-tale, why not death? Yeah, I could get killed by a bus, and I'd be in the same boat - no last words, no closure. Death is random no matter what you're dying from, I guess.

Should I look for the silver lining instead?

> *A heart, full of joy and gladness*
> *Will always banish sadness and strife*
> *So always look for the silver lining*
> *And try to find the sunny side of life*
> *That song is a load of crap!*

Look, I've tried. Maybe I can't muster the Pollyanna in me because she wasn't there to begin with…. I can't remember. However, I am grateful for the simple pleasures; things we take for granted, like breath. In and out… inhale… exhale. It happens without thinking, minute by minute, hour by hour - day in, day out. Have you ever considered that you could forget to breathe? Let that sink in for a moment. Forget. To. Breathe. It's unimaginable. I can't **wrap** my head around any of it.

The good news is, by the time my brain shrivels to the size of a prune, I'll no longer be concerned with mundane things like eating, or breathing. But, there's still hope… I could die from the big C or a massive clot that lodges mercifully in a lung. Hey… there's the silver lining. And you didn't think I had it in me.

Oh, Rainey, you always see the bright side, don't you sweetheart? **You** *are my Pollyanna. My head might forget you, but my heart never will!*

Oh, Al, you're an unfeeling, uncaring scourge from hell!

LIFE CALLING

Beep. This is Dr. Bennett's office calling again. Please give us a ring as soon as possible to re-schedule your appointment. Thank you. Beep.

Beep. I'm calling from Dr. Bennett's office. You missed your last appointment. It's critical you contact the office and re-schedule as soon as possible. Thank you. Beep.

Beep. Hello. This is Dr. Brigette Bennett. I'm concerned. You've missed your last appointment with me, and two with Ms. Velasquez. Please call me as soon as you get this message, otherwise, I'll have no choice but to contact your next of kin. Thanks. Beep.

Dr. Who? Bennett? Oh shit! Wait, a minute… uh… Is he that guy with the unibrow?

Not unless Brigitte has gender issues, you idiot!

Hold on. I'm sure I have her card in my purse. No, no. No talkie to the kids; that's my job.

My entire existence revolves around appointments, tests, specialists, pharmacies, hospitals, clinics, repeat, repeat, repeat. Shit. I can't remember the last time I did anything else. I used to... well, do... things, now I can't muster enough motivation to fart.

The reality is I've lost interest in most everything - books, people... life; stuck in a medical orbit - going around and around and around, until I crash and burn. How exciting, life by rote.

Ah, here it is... Dr. Bennett, Geriatric Psychiatrist. Geriatric, my ass, and why do I need a psychiatrist for Christ's sake? If I need analysis, my personal psycho-babbler is available.

God forbid we're not politically correct. Why don't they call it what it really is, Psychiatry for the Decrepit?

What does she want with me, anyway? It's not like she's helping, and I'm sick to death of taxing my brain. Won't that make me sicker? "Try not to stress." What a joke! What do you think you guys are doing, giving me a spa day?

I swear, doctors would continue testing and giving us meds after we were cold and dead if they could. Helping you live longer? Bullshit! They're not remedying, they're compiling statistics. When they say, "prolonged life," they mean by hours, or days. Patient, "Sorry You're Fucked," survived three weeks longer than the median."

Marvellous, a medical miracle… toss in another, Ambien. Whoopee!

Did I tell you, they asked me to donate my brain? I think they meant after I'm dead, but who can tell with these Frankensteins? What in hell will they learn from this soon to be pea-brain? By the time I kick off, there won't be enough brain left to see shit. If they really want to learn something, they should remove it now; a win-win?

Would you be keen on that, Al, being chopped up, dissected? Now you know how I feel.

A life dictated by disease and doctors is not a pleasant combo. It's tiresome. I used to be a person, now I'm a statistic; which is why I'm choosing not to disclose Al's presence. It's bad enough the white coats treat me like an Auschwitz survivor, do I need that from my family too? It would be… dehumanizing.

I recall how degraded and insignificant people felt once their diagnosis was revealed. And now…the moment we've all been waiting for… The star of the show? Cancer! (Applause, applause.) Guest starring… whoooooo… cares?

You're no longer… human; you're the dying one, the sick one, the poor one, the pitied one. Once word gets out, you're Blah with cancer, or Blah with, Al… or Poor, Blah. Suddenly, you exist in some alternate universe; and, the shift is abrupt and tragic... and fatal. Once you enter the realm of the death and dying, there's no turning back. Even if you survive by some miracle, you will always be, Blah that had...

"Hello? Yes, I had a message from Dr. Bennett about a missed appointment? I'm sorry. I did notify the office I was away."

Shut up. I have to lie.

"I'm afraid we didn't get the message, but you must keep your appointments. Dr. Bennett is very busy. Also, Ms. Velasquez needs to schedule a home visit."

Well, pardon me all to hell! I didn't realize the world revolved around Dr. Bennett's schedule! Fuck her!

"Ms. Velasquez?"

"She's the O.T.? - The Occupational Therapist?

"Oh, yes. I remember. Well, I'm sorry, but I'm still away."

"When will you be returning?"

"That's the thing, I'm out of the country; on a vacation-work thing with my son."

"It's vital you... Can you hold, please?"

"Sure."

I have oodles of time to listen to, Girl from Ipanema, the elevator version. What's next, Lawrence Welk?

"Hello. This is Dr. Bennett. I'm concerned, the Alzhei..."

"Yes!... Yes, but I'm doing fine... and..."

"... may be progressing."

"I'm with my son. I'm fine."

"I'm glad to hear it, however you need to come in. I'm booking an appointment for you next week."

"But, I just told you, I'm out of the country."

"Perhaps I could speak with your son and explain how important..."

"That won't be necessary. Give me a second."

Fuck! Fuck! Fuck! Where's that bloody pen? Fuck!

"Okay, go ahead."

"Monday the fifth at ten a.m. If you don't come in, I will have no choice but to contact your family."

"I'll tell him, but he won't be happy."

"I can speak with him and explain the circumstances if you like?"

"No. That wont' be necessary."

"You **have** discussed your diagnosis, and treatment with them, have you not?

"Of course, I have."

"Good. It would be beneficial if one of them could accompany you on your next visit?"

"My daughter's out of the country, and my son is extremely busy at work. He's got a new job, so I don't think that will be possible."

"Can you bring someone with you, perhaps a friend?"

"I'll see who's free."

"All right. See you on the fifth."

What did I tell you about, life with, Al? Doctors, doctors, doctors! Ugh.

Beep. Hi, it's Mary. Just calling to say hello. Everybody misses you at choir. The soprano section isn't the same without you. Hope everything is going well. Okay, I'll try again soon. Love to the family. Beep.

Beep. Hello. I'm calling from Minute Lube. You had an appointment booked with us for an oil change and a tire rotation? Let us know when you'd like to reschedule. Thanks. Beep.

Beep. It's me again. How's Tuesday for coffee, say two-ish? Beep.

Beep. Hi, it's Sandy from C.T. Bank. Just wanted to inform you you're overdrawn on your account. Please call me - 293-242-5941. We can work something out. Thanks, Bye. Beep.

Beep. Mum? Are you there? It's Meg. Raine and I want to swing by for a visit today. Let me know. Thanks. Bye. Beep.

Beep. This is Paul Durcan from Hydro Central. Your payment is past due. If you're struggling at the moment, we can offer options. Call me at 293-462-9785. Thanks. Beep.

Beep. It's Jean. This is message number three, kiddo. If I don't hear from you, I'm coming in with the Mounties. Call me. Beep.

LEAVE ME ALONE!

MAYBE THE PHONE RANG

"Unfortunately, there's no definitive test for Alzheimer's, but we can make an educated guess by a process of elimination. We'll make an appointment for an MRI to assess shrinkage, and rule out other conditions such as tumours, stroke or head injury."

"Shrinkage? Shrinkage of what?"

"Your brain."

Bwa-ha-ha-ha. It will get smaller and smaller until it's the size of a walnut! Ha-ha-ha!

Oh, my God, my brain will shrink?

"Then, we'll send you for a PET Scan. No need to worry about the radiation, it's a small dose... Barely enough to kill a small Ontario town.

190

Wouldn't it be more humane if you killed me with the radiation?

"If it's Alzheimer's, there is a variety of drugs that can slow the...

Excruciating, brain shrinking, signal halting, plaque depositing process, down.

"Slow it down? So, there's no cure?"

"Cure?"

Ha-ha-ha! I'm afraid not. But, we'll give you medications, and diapers...

"Blah, blah blah; wah, wah, wah."

No cure... No cure... No cure... No cure... No cure.

Please stop saying that!

No cure... No cure... No cure.

You'll see specialist upon specialist, it'll make your head spin!

"They'll assess memory and cognitive abilities; in the meantime, try not to worry. I'd like to reiterate your symptoms can be the result of several things...

Who are we kidding? We know what this is, but we want to drag the torture out for as long as possible.

Try not to worry? Are you kidding me? No cure, no cure, no cure, no cure, no cure.

"Are all these tests necessary? Didn't you say, you might be jumping the gun?"

"I realize it can be a little overwhelming..."

Like breathing under water, or jumping from a plane with no parachute... but the faster we get a diagnosis, the sooner we can sedate you to where you won't be able to discern whether you're awake or asleep.

"Here, take these pamphlets."

Early treatment is essential so you can:

1) Plan for the future

2) Take care of financial and legal matters

3) Address potential safety issues

4) Learn about living arrangements

5) Take part in clinical trials

Isn't it counterintuitive to plan for a non-existent future?

"You should speak to your family; having a good support system is very important...

For when you shit in your shorts. Ha-ha-ha.

"Yes. Yes, thank you."

Like hell! You want me to worry my kids because I'm getting a little forgetful? Not a chance!

Cool it, brainless. It's not the doctor's fault!

So, what! Shoot the damn messenger; she signed the death warrant!

Okay, I may not have a perfect recollection of that day, so as Ripley used to say, Believe it, or not!

I had every one of those bloody tests - white cone in the black hole, blue square in the red space; what's your name, where were you born, what year is it? Blah, blah, blah. And, I saw every one of those brainiac specialists; gerontologist, psychotherapist, and a few other "ists."

The despair was crushing; similar to being part of the Dead Child's Club. I'm talking, utter bleakness; the kind of desolation where you scrape your way up from the deepest well, only to realize you must then climb Everest, to spelunk an even bigger mountain, before you can see daybreak … and there it was… light bulb. Why do I have to wait for, Al to finish the job? I can end it right now.

I lined those babies up; white, blue, purple, brown, yellow; enough pills to obliterate the neighbourhood…

I could lie and tell you I had an epiphany, or chickened out, when I realized my action would trap me in purgatory for eternity; or I felt pangs of guilt for leaving my family in grief, or even that I… changed my mind. But… the truth is… I forgot. Maybe the phone rang, or some kid showed up at the door selling Girl Guide cookies… I don't know. I swallowed my regular dose of listless and depressing and carried on. The good news was, at least I wasn't able to sleep.

At least my sarcasm still works.

All those pills ever did was give me insomnia, constipation and vertigo. I stumbled around like a drunk on a bender. I did a real number on my shins once, falling up the stairs Yeah, you heard me; **up** the stairs! My leg was black for weeks. I told the kids I tripped; they simply weren't in on the specifics.

The pretty yellow tablet constipated me to the point, I couldn't crap for a month. I looked like I'd just come from a hot dog eating contest and was ready to blow!

Nope, nope, nope! Don't even go there! I'm in no mood for pee or poo jokes!

I kept all those lovely tablets tucked away where no one would find them; played the game of where shall I hide them today? Such fun! The bathroom was out of the question; way too obvious! The kitchen? Mmm, nope... same problem. And when the old hat box at the top of the closet became impossible because dizziness kept me from climbing on the stool, I resorted to keeping them under my mattress. I moved them from the bedroom a while ago, because Kooky Cookie's daughter was stealing my pillowcases, and I was terrified she'd find them.

Al told me she was stealing. He's such a bloody snitch!

It's exhausting keeping secrets. I know, I know... at some point, I need to disclose the nasty details; or as my grandmother used to say, spill the beans. I'm just not ready. For the moment, I'm choosing to postpone the pity party indefinitely.

When will you be ready? When you're dead?

Shut-up, Al, you're Persona non grata, remember?

Where are those pills, anyway?

Who cares? They were as effective as hairspray in a tornado! I've been taking them for a zillion years and am I better? NO!

Al's still sucking away the brain juice. Although... I could use a Lorah–something right about now. I haven't slept in... days? Months? Years? **Why can't I remember?**

*You know why, shit for brains. That, and the fact you're **not sleeping**. And don't be pissy. Al thrives on pissiness.*

Shit, Al, back off! You're exhausting me, you son of a bitch! I hate you! Do you hear me? I HATE YOU!

Why don't you just kill me already?

I HATE YOU, DOUG CARROLL

Mummy and Baba painted my furniture all white and gold while I was away at camp; now my bedroom looks like a fairy princess land. We moved to a new house this summer, and I love it; I even have my own room, with a desk that looks right into the backyard. No pigeons here, ha-ha-ha, and it doesn't smell like pee.

My room is on the second floor, and we have three bathrooms! I've never lived in a house that had an upstairs before, and the best part, is that right around the corner, there's a place called, Sherwood Park; like the forest in Robin Hood. It's so big, it takes hours to walk from one end of the park to the other. I know, 'cause I timed it one day.

I love riding down the gigantic hill. I take my feet off the pedals and fly… The wind makes my face tingle, like when you walk through a snowstorm on a cold, windy day.

The slides, swings, monkey bars, and these plastic house things you can hide in like a fort, are all at the bottom of the hill. There's a jungle gym, a big sandbox, and even a gigantic maze, but not like the ones you get lost in. I think it's called a labyrinth. Oh, and, you can swim at the park too; well, not really swim; it's more for babies. You kinda walk around and getting squirted. I don't like it, 'cause the concrete is rough and the water is too cold. I don't know why babies like it.

The swings are ginormous. They're the kind with a big, 'U,' seat where your bum hangs out the back? Once, my leg got pinched inside the S things that attach to the leather. That happens when you don't sit **right** in the middle! Sometimes I get queasy swinging, but last week it wasn't bothering for some reason, so I started swinging really hard. I kicked and kicked, and tried going over the top, but it was too hard. You'd need a monster or something to push you over.

At the far end, there's a teeter-totter; but I can't get on, 'cause usually I'm by myself. Even when someone helped me on once, my feet couldn't touch the ground; and then the stupid kid on the other end got yanked off, and crash went my butt into the dirt. It killed.

Past the Jungle Jim, there're these old wooden stairs; like a thousand of them? After you climb to the top, the park disappears; that's how high you are. There is a million, billion paths up here, but you have to be careful, 'cause if you trip on the big tree roots that stick out of the ground, you could fall a long, long way. You could even die! Yeah, there's lots of dangerous things here.

Sometimes, when I get tired of riding my bike or playing, I climb to the top and write. At school, I always get an A in writing. There's a spot where no one goes… it's my secret place. I pretend I'm a sea captain or a girl captured by mountain ogres. My favourite pretend game is being in the jungle surrounded by shrunken heads. Mummy says, "sometimes I worry about you, kid! Why do you always write about shrunken heads?" She's joking; sort of. I guess I just like writing scary stuff.

When I grow up, I'm going to be an actress or a writer. I could be both, because Mummy says I can be anything I set my mind to.

Sometimes, I bring, Jimmy to the park - he's my next-door neighbour. He's only six, but he has two older brothers; Russell and Doug. I like Doug a lot! He's a fifteen-year-old genius! One time, he showed me how to pick a lock, like Al Mundy does in our favourite show, It Takes A Thief.

"Show me, Doug."

"Okay, but don't tell anyone."

"I won't."

"Promise?"

"I promise... I promise!"

"You need these special picks. I keep mine in this velvet wrap, and no one knows about them, so if you tell, I'll kill you."

"I won't. Does Russell know?"

"NO. Nobody knows, not even my brothers."

"Okay, open the lock."

"Wow, that's cool. Let me try."

"Ha-ha. Forget it."

"Please? Come on!"

"No!"

"Why not?"

"You've gotta be a genius, like me, and a man. You're just a stupid girl."

"I am not. And girls are smart too, you know! Come on... Show me!"

"No!"

"Hey, Doug? Do you want to kiss me?"

"What? NO! Eww."

"I hate you, Doug Carroll!"

"Ha-ha-ha… Ooooh. You think I care?"

I did hate him too… for a second.

Sometimes, I wait outside in the backyard, hoping he'll come out so we can talk. I don't mind the cold, and when the moon is out, it's so beautiful against the winter branches. Doug usually comes out after supper, even when it's foggy or snowing. He knows I wait for him. I don't think he has many friends, at least I never see any.

Baba hates Doug and Russell because they ride their bikes over her flowers and smush them. She yells at them to stop, but they stick their tongues out at her and laugh.

"If dey done stop, we gonna move."

"Oh, no… No, please, Baba. I don't want to leave. I love it here so much. And what about Sherwood Park? It's my favourite place in the world."

"I done care. You tell him stop, or else we gonna move. Dis not good for my nerve."

"Okay, Baba."

"Doug Carroll, you need to stop riding your bike all over my grandmother's flowers."

"Why, what's she gonna do if I don't?"

"She said, we'll have to move, that's what."

"So, what do I care? Your grandmother's an old bat."

"Don't you even care if I move away?"

"No. Why should I?"

"I hate you, Doug Carroll!"

Baba told Mummy she hates, Fay too; that's Doug's mom.

"Dat woman has da men coming all da time. She's a whore!"

Mummy gave her that look like - Geez, Ma, not in front of the kid! But I'm twelve now. I'm not a baby anymore.

I'm gonna remember this place forever...

Is Doug is picking my brain?

AESOP AND OTHER FABLES

"A whore? Ha-ha-ha. What a lovely story Mother."

"What?"

"You were on some jag about a park, a whore; secrets, something?"

"Sorry, I was... reminiscing; apparently, out loud."

"About a prostitute? Um, okay."

"I've been reminiscing a lot about the past lately; places I used to live, your dad, stuff that happened to you and David when you were little."

"It's okay to look back briefly, but don't dwell in the past, Mother, you can make yourself melancholy. Remember... the past is past, the future's the future, but today's a gift, that's why it's called, the present?"

"Oh, come on. I hope this kind of banal platitude isn't in your book."

"Ha-ha-ha. So, what should we talk about?"

"Up to you."

"Well, sounds like you had some interesting adventures."

"I had a life, pre-David, and Paige, so yes, I had a few adventures."

"Tell me some."

"What? Right now?"

"Why not? Do you have a previous engagement? A public speaking event, perhaps?"

"Very funny."

"All right, let's see… well, I stole a chocolate bar once."

"**A whole bar?**"

"There's no need for sarcasm, Paige."

"Ha-ha. How old were you?"

"Maybe... nine? Your grandmother figured I'd stolen it because I had no money. Of course, she made me return it to the store and apologize to the owner."

"That's your adventure?"

"You're right... more of an Aesop Fable; but there were other things."

"Such as?"

"I'd tell you, but as the adage goes; I'd have to kill you."

"Oh, come on, Mother. There has to be some juicy tid-bit you can share?"

"Oh, Paige, for heaven's sake, I can't remember off the top of my head. I'll give it some thought and get back to you."

"Mother? Do you ever miss being married; sex?"

"**Paige**!"

"What? That's a legitimate question. You've been alone a long time since dad died."

"How odd. I've thought about your dad more in the last two days, than I have in twenty years. Do you remember him, Paige?"

"Some."

"How old were you, I can't remember?"

"I was ten, I had nightmares for the longest time, but not about dad; about seeing you all covered in blood. You looked like a victim in a horror film."

"I can't picture his face anymore. Even when I see photographs, he doesn't seem real; as if he never existed. Oh, but there was one thing I remembered, the man couldn't tell a joke to save his life. Ha-ha. Strange the things that come to mind."

"So, do you miss it?"

"What? Being married?"

"Marriage, intimacy? You're still young, Mother. Do you ever… date?"

"Oh, gosh. Not anymore, but I wasn't a hermit"

"I don't remember any men hanging around."

"The cardinal rule of motherhood; never introduce your dates to your kids until it's serious. I didn't want to be perceived as, a Fay."

"Who?"

206

"The woman I was mumbling about? Never mind. Anyway, there was no one I was serious enough with to allow you and David to know about."

"I can't fathom in all these years there hasn't been anyone special. They couldn't have all been hook-ups?"

"What?"

"Flings?"

"Paige, some things should be private. Discretion really is the better part of valour."

"Mother, I'm a grown woman, and a professional. I can handle a steamy tale."

"Oh, Michael, I can't do this anymore. I'm sure he suspects."

"Tell him."

"I can't. It would crush him. He doesn't deserve that."

"What about what you? Don't you deserve happiness? Leave him."

"I can't."

"Can't, or won't?"

"It's easy for you; no attachments, you come and go as you please. What about the kids? This would scar them for life, and Paige already hates me."

"I love you."

"Oh, my darling; if only that was enough. We escape into a beautiful, enjoyable fantasy, but we must live in reality; and the reality is that breaking up a marriage is messy and painful."

"Your marriage is already broken... Isn't your mantra; love conquers all? You've always told me that love is enough - please let it be enough."

"Michael... it's not that simple."

"Are you happy?"

"Happy? Happiness is an impractical transitory emotion, it changes like the wind."

"How can you say that? Happiness is everything."

"That's where we differ, my love. Euphoria is fleeting. I have a home, kids; I can't throw everyone's life into chaos on a selfish decision."

"What about, our life?"

"We don't have a life."

"So, the two years means nothing to you?"

"Oh, Michael. Don't play the injured paramour. This isn't Hollywood, my love - there are no happy endings. And please don't act desperate, it doesn't suit you. I do love you, but it can't last."

"Why not?"

"Because nothing ever does."

"Hello… Earth to Mother?"

"What?"

"I said I can handle a steamy tale."

Well, you're not getting one. Anyway, what are you doing here; how come you're not in Timbuktu?"

"I finished up last night. I told you I'd be dropping by today."

"You most certainly did not!"

"Yes, Mother, I did. We talked about it, remember? You asked me to come on Wednesday, and I told you I was still away, so you said Thursday would be fine.

Thursday? Is that after Monday? After… Tuesday? Wait… before, Sunday?

"I'm sure I'd remember if you said you were coming."

Really? We'd remember? Ha-ha-ha.

"Well, you didn't. Do you want me to leave?"

"No. In fact, I'd like you to stay. I want to show you something. Come with me."

"Here… I want you to have this."

"What is it?"

"Open it."

"The cross your mother gave you when you were born?"

"Yes, and now, I want you to pass it on to your daughter."

"Okay, but that could be a while. What's the rush?"

"What's wrong with now?"

"Well, I hate to state the obvious Mother, but I don't have kids, and for…

"What about, Raine?"

"What about her?"

"She's old enough to have this."

"Yes, but Raine isn't mine."

"What?"

"Raine?... She's David's child - David and Meg?"

"I know that! I meant she's **like** a daughter to you! You are her Godmother. It would be a lovely gift coming from you. But... if you give this to Raine, what will you give your own daughter?"

"When the time comes, I'm sure I'll find something."

"What time?"

"When I have a child, Mother! Isn't that what we're talking about? What's wrong with you?"

"**Nothing is wrong with me.** I thought it would be a nice gesture that's all!"

If she doesn't want to give it to her daughter, fine! And who the hell is, Meg? She's not that woman who's always smiling, is she?

WOMAN PLANS, GOD LAUGHS

Is the cat out of the bag? Is my shrinking brain attracting attention? Something's going on because D's been trying to make play dates with me; even Raine is in on the act.

I don't want them here; they're stealing things. That smiling mannequin of a wife is the worst. Pots, cutlery, gardening tools? All disappeared. She can't waltz in here and take whatever she pleases. This is David's fault. There'll be no more dating her; he's grounded!

Yeah, your brain is shrinking... like the one in your maudlin stories.

Fuck off! Stop reminding me. You're like a nail gun on a two by four!

D, bought me a wall-sized calendar for my kitchen and filled it in for me. He says he did it, so it would be easier for me to see, in case I can't find my glasses. As Sherlock

Holmes says, the game's afoot. He doesn't want me forgetting Raine's birthday. Pfff, as if.

Wait, a minute! He suspects? You've told him, haven't you, Al? You son of a bitch, if you breathe a word, I'll... I'll... Was it, Dr. Bitch? She said she'd keep everything confidential. I knew she was a liar - they all are - every one.

I'll admit the calendar is convenient. Here it is in big red marker; Raine, June 27th. Okay, so what? Who doesn't forget things? I'm only human. I didn't forget Raine loves my brownies, so I'm making her a big batch for her birthday, and, I've ordered her something very special. They're coming all the way from England. Paige helped me place the order on the Internet. I hope they get here on time.

I used to manage the computer quite well, once upon a time, but it's all so perplexing now. And what the hell is it with books these days? The minuscule print and the stories... have they gotten dull, or is it just me and my addled brain? Don't answer that.

Come on... let it go.

Oh... how freeing, but I can't, not yet. Just a little longer. A little... longer.

Did I mention Raine loves art? She's exceptionally talented. When I was her age, I could barely draw a line.

Isn't it interesting how each of us has different gifts? I used to wonder what my purpose for living was, until I heard someone say, find your gift and use it to make the world a better place.

What did you ever do to make the world a better place you selfish cow?

I… I… don't remember, but I must have done something. I could be doing it right now.

The only thing you're doing right now is shrinking.

No! No… I'm still loving. That's everything, isn't it? Love?

Yeah… it's easy to love the people that love you. What about what's her name; the blatherer?

Stop it! Forgive me. Forgive me, Lord. I'm sorry. This won't keep me from entering Heaven, will it?

I'm convinced we arrive on this planet aware of who we are, but minute by minute, year by year, life's abrasions dissolve us; erode our senses; confound, delude, dupe. By the end, we're all frauds.

You don't help, Al… twisting and contorting the truths of my life. I don't know what's real anymore.

I can't remember the last time I had clarity. Everything is topsy-turvy, muddled, confused; black - white, white - black, and fifty shades of gray.

Why does that sound familiar?

We realize we need to unlearn, undo, and unravel everything the world cultivated in us, in order to get back to the person we started out as; our authentic selves.

Because life is one big gaslight.

Hey, Al, why don't you gobble the lying parts; the chunks that are hypocritical and judgmental? Why don't you grind away the masks; the pretense; the biases and hatred and leave the good stuff? Is it necessary to gorge it all? You're a pig! I HATE YOU, YOU ASSHOLE!

Abundant riches await on the horizon...

All aboard, The Golden Years... going nowhere.

This is the time to forgive, to heal, unburden, release sorrow; a final chance to seize the fullness of life, not have it snatched, chewed and shrunken away. I'm not coming into my own, I'm... be-coming. Dammit! It's not fair! **It's not fair!**

The sun rises in the morning, and sets in the... Clouds bring wind? The earth traverses the sun every... six hundred days?

215

Words, sentences, thoughts, all slip-sliding away. God, even my own thoughts are non-sequiturs! Why am I talking about the fucking weather?

Oh, Raine... I won't see you grow up. I won't hear all about the Prom. I'll never meet your first beau, or tell you how beautiful and grown-up you look.

Raine has a lovely beau. I think his name is David. Perhaps he'll be at the party. No one uses the word, beau anymore or even, boyfriend, do they? There's another word - sounds like someone in a law firm? Anyway, that's all besides the point, because... because... Uh... I'm sorry, lost my train of thought.

I think Gays confused me; and no, I'm not homophobic. It's just... I can barely remember the letters in my own name, and they've used every bloody letter in the alphabet, including the Q. Geez! And is it true that we now genderless? Aren't breasts still female? And vaginas? Oh, Lord... I **am** losing my mind. Good, God! Soon, we'll all be letters. A, for athlete, C, for cook? Those of us, Al affected will be, AD; addle-brained for short. I might be getting out before the world goes completely to shit! Silver Lining? For myself, perhaps, but my kids still have to inhabit this planet. I don't envy the problems they'll face; the garbage, pollution.

But how will they fix anything if they only address each other by, They, or, Them, or It? I guess they'll figure it out

216

with code or something. Tomorrow's problems will take care of themselves, as they say.

There's always a balance between good and bad, so, I'm praying there'll be medical miracles. Splicing and dicing genes might save the next generation from many horrors; Cancer, M.S., depression? Only time will tell.

They will stop you, Al! At least I hope they will because I couldn't bear to think of Rainey… my sweet, sweet, Rainey…

Oh, no! **No. No! NO!** *Rule number one! Rule number…*

Who am I talking to, anyway?

Hello? *Is anyone there?*

Why are my cheeks wet?

NOBODY HOME

"David, I've tried calling your mom to tell her you're on the way, but no one's answering."

"She's probably outside waiting for me."

"Okay, but don't be long; everyone's coming for three."

"Back in a jiff!"

"Ma, it's me... Hello? Ma, pick up... I'm out front."

"Hello-o? It's party time. Ma? Hey, come on, we're going to be late. Ma? Are you here? Ma!"

Ugh... Why is the power off?

"Hey, Meg, did Ma call by any chance?"

"No, why?"

"I'm at the house, and she's not."

"What do you mean?"

"I mean, she isn't here; I can't find her, and the power is off. Nothing's working."

"Where could she be, a neighbour's? Is the power off in the entire area?"

"I can't tell. Anyway, she wouldn't have gone next door."

"Why not?"

"Long story. I'm going around back, hold on… The car's in the garage, but I don't see her. My stomach is churning. What the hell could have happened."

"Don't panic, David. I'm sure there's a logical… Oh…

"What?"

"You don't think she wandered off, do you?"

"What do you mean, like she decided it was time for a stroll?"

219

"You know what I mean."

"Christ, Meg. Not this again!"

"Okay, fine, fine. You're probably right; she has to be around. What do you want to do?"

"I'm not sure. If she doesn't turn up in a few minutes, I'll drive over to the grocery. Maybe she needed to pick up something last minute."

"I'm sure that's it. What do you want me to do?"

"Go ahead with the party. We don't want to spoil it for Raine."

"Yeah, okay - call me if you find her; **when** you find her."

"K, bye."

Shhh. Someone's in the house.

Oh, God... It's my neighbour with her poison... She won't find me in the barrel.

AT LEAST IT'S NOT FEBRUARY

"When did you last speak to her, sir?"

"This morning."

"And you told her you were coming?"

"Yes. I said I'd pick her up at two forty-five."

"Does she drive?"

"Yes, but I checked, and the car's in the garage."

"Would she go to a neighbour, or a friend's?"

"I don't think so.

"Is it possible she... wandered off?"

"Honestly? I'm not sure."

"Has she done anything like this before?"

"No… Never."

"Excuse me. I need to get this, it's my wife."

"Hello?"

"So, what's happening?"

"The police are here; we're just going over details."

"David, it's best if you and Paige handle this. We'll continue with the party."

"That's a good idea, Meg. Dear God, I hope we don't need to get into this with Raine."

"I agree. Call me the second you know anything!"

"I will. Gotta go!"

"Sorry, Officer.

"Does your mother have any mental impairment, like dementia or Alzheimer's?"

"No."

"… Um, she might."

"Paige!"

"Sorry, David. I think we should work on that premise for now, okay?"

"If that's the case, it's imperative we find her. Is there any special place she likes to go, a coffee shop, library - anywhere like that?"

"The only place she might go is church."

"Where's that?

"It's Crystal United, on the corner of Crystal Terrace and Acre."

"We'll check it out."

"Do you know what she was wearing? Colour of her coat that sort of thing?"

"No! We didn't coordinate our outfits for Christ's sake! This is ridiculous! Something has happened to my mother, and…

"Sir, stay calm. I realize this is distressing, but in most cases, the individual has forgotten about the event and gone elsewhere. Do you have any recent photographs of your mother?"

"Uh, yeah. She's changed a little since I took this; grayer and thinner, but you'll be able to recognize her."

"We'll canvas the neighbourhood, but I would suggest you call her friends. We see this all the time. The person usually turns up with a good explanation; they forgot; got the dates mixed-up. If it's something else, we'll find her; we're lucky it's June and not February. Try not to worry."

"Oh, God."

"It's all right David, we'll find her. She's on foot, so..."

"Why the hell would she go anywhere?"

"Oh, come on, Paige. Don't give me that look!"

"David… Why don't you sit down? I'll get Mother's address book and call around."

"All of Mother's friends said the same thing, they haven't seen her. Jean Tarchuck told me that Mother dropped out of choir and hasn't been to church in almost seven months. The last time they spoke, she said, Mother seemed distant; depressed. Jean tried to set up a coffee date, but every time she called, Mother made some excuse why they couldn't meet. Her friends said it's like she fell off the face of the earth."

"Meg said the day she was helping Ma find her keys, she found the answering machine unplugged, and Ma nearly took her head off when she plugged it back in. She said there were a ton of messages, but Ma wouldn't listen to them."

"Let's listen to them now."

"We can't, the power's out."

"Paige? Look at this. There's nothing in the fridge except stale milk."

"David? There're months worth of unpaid bills here, including several from Hydro. This explains why her power is off. How long has she been living like this?"

"I don't know."

"This is pretty clear, David."

"No, you're wrong. I can't even say it."

"Apparently, neither can she. Come on, David, open your eyes! She's forgetful, losing things; she's accused Meg of stealing, she's gotten lost driving? And no wonder she hasn't invited anyone over, look at the state of this house? Even you can't ignore this. It all makes sense. Last time I visited, she was rambling about some park, then insisted, Raine was my daughter."

"David, why didn't you tell me there was more to this than Mother misplacing keys and talking to herself? Did you want to keep it a secret? This is nothing to be ashamed of."

"I'm not ashamed, Paige, I…

"What? What then? You won't talk about it; you won't even consider the possibility that's she's going senile. Every time the subject is mentioned, you shut the conversation down."

"She's our mother, Paige! She's my… Ma, okay? I can't bear….

"All right… take a breath. Let's focus on finding her; we can sort the rest out later. Don't worry, I'll take care of everything. There are excellent doctors…

"Oh, **now** you waltz in and want to take care of everything? How wonderful! Paige steps in and saves the day."

"David!"

"You can't matter-of-factly swoop in and be the hero; Paige, the renowned psycho babbler, saves the day! Where's your cape? Fuck!"

"It's been brutal - the new job; Meg and I fighting every day."

"Why didn't you call, David?"

"Why was it up to me? You could have picked up the phone? My, God, you never check in. She's your mother too!"

"David...

"Oh, God... I'm sorry, Paige. I'm not angry with you; I'm pissed with myself. This is all my fault. If I'd...

"That's ridiculous, David. You couldn't prevent Mother's dementia."

"Yeah, but I wasn't paying attention. Meg kept telling me something was wrong, and I kept dismissing her. I buried myself in work, and when I got home, I told myself I was too tired to deal with the situation. But my gut? I've been a coward, Paige. I was so afraid of the truth, but if I'd seen it sooner...

"David, if it's any consolation, I didn't want to see it either; but we're jumping the gun. We don't know anything yet, at least not definitively... but, I'm sorry too. I'm sorry I wasn't here for you; for you and Meg. I can see you've been under a terrible strain."

"To be honest, I did use my job as an excuse - not consciously, but I suspected something was off. Mother and I lock horns on everything, so I chose to stay on the periphery. She's always been closer to you and Meg, anyway. She wouldn't accept my help even if I was here; stubborn woman. Ugh! But, I could have helped you and Meg... and I will."

"If Ma has dementia, maybe she won't remember you don't get along?"

"Oh, ho-ho… funny."

"Hey… laughing-crying… It's a fine line, right?"

"Yeah… but all kidding aside… I'm here now, David; please let me help. We'll get through this, I promise."

"We just have to find her."

THIS LONESOME VALLEY

Jesus walked this lonesome valley
He had to walk it by himself
O, nobody else could walk it for him
He had to walk it by himself

I've always loved this hymn; but until recently I didn't understand the depth of loneliness Jesus felt; and the valley grows darker every day. How lonely the dying... No words can articulate the depths of isolation, fear, and uncertainty that the dying suffer; one foot in this plane, the other in the unknown.

We can walk beside them, but we can't take their pain, or die for them, can we? We stand at the abyss, but as long as we're tethered to life, we can't take the plunge.

This is new territory. Having, Al is like being attached to a bungee cord; the brain plunges, but the body gets yanked back from the brink. Jump, repeat, jump, repeat, jump, repeat, until... splat.

One day, we'll stare into that vacuous hole, and belly flop; but not today. Hell, I won't even be aware I'm dying; at least I don't think 1 will. Al will destroy command central, and that will be that; brain-dead... body dead.

*I hear you whispering inside my head. You won't succeed turning me into you. I am not a disease, and I will never allow you to define me. What's that old saying? We don't **have** a soul, we **are** a soul? As much as you chew and suck the life juice from my head, you can't destroy **me**.*

We've had a misunderstanding, you and I, Al. I've always thought you were out to get me, that you were making me feel weak, vulnerable, not good enough, kind enough, loving enough. But you aren't doing that, are you? All this time... it's been me. I finally understand. It's not personal, is it, Al? It was never personal. You don't hate me, you're just doing your job; like a virus or bacteria? You can't change your nature, any more than I can mine. Wow! All this energy wasted fighting an imaginary foe. Well... that's all over. Done. Finished. And you know what? I'm not afraid anymore.

The "Way of the warrior is resolute acceptance of death." I can't remember who said this, but whoever you are... kudos - you nailed it!

Life is a Proverb. When you think about it, it's all the Proverbs. The one I remember is: if God is for us, who can be against us? This verse from Romans encompasses, Al, the big C, and every and all circumstances that challenge us in life.

Why didn't faith sustain me or propel me into a place of peace right from the get-go? I don't know. Perhaps, it's a requirement to experience the prerequisite stages of denial, anger, bargaining and depression before arriving at acceptance? I've poo-pooed the notion of free will, but I can see now, the debate has merit.

I'm unclear as to whether God gets frustrated or amused by the fact that we make life so complicated, but I'm not going to beat myself up for allowing fear to overshadow faith. After all, I'm only human. Maybe, less human than I used to be - or perhaps more so, because I've come to understand I am more than the sum of my parts? More human... less human? Ugh... I don't know - anyway, just theory.

We talked about things that aren't quantifiable, didn't we? Well, if we didn't, let me assure you, there are, and I myself am an unquantifiable entity. While science can define blood and bone, tissue and sinew; even Al isn't understood completely. And the greatest minds have yet to fathom the soul.

I'm certain an alternate dimension exists; one that can't be explained; not yet, at least. Hey, dimension - dementia? Is it possible that we need to rid ourselves of our brains to glean Heaven? Anyway, the only way to understand death is to die. "Ay, there's the rub." Some Shakespearean uttered those words; however, you'll need to look up who; I'll be damned if I can remember.

So, fear be damned. Mummy, are you waiting for me?

Mummy... I'm not scared anymore.

> *I must go and stand my trial*
> *I have to stand it by myself*
> *O, nobody else can stand it for me*
> *I have to stand it by myself.*

I'm ready...

SO, IT BEGINS

"Well, she's dehydrated and as you might expect, a little confused. We'll keep her overnight just to be sure she's okay."

"Any idea what's wrong?"

"Other than dehydration, and her current condition, there doesn't seem to be anything major; no head trauma, just some minor bumps and bruises. All things considered, she's doing well. I'll be sure to let Dr. Bennett know."

"In the meantime, we'll take excellent care of you, won't we?"

"Try not to worry, she's in good hands."

"Who is Dr. Bennett?"

"Your mom's primary physician? Brigitte Bennett?"

"What about, Susan Tarrin?"

"She's her mom's G.P., but since her diagnosis, she's been seeing Brigette Bennett. She's the resident Geriatric Psychotherapist."

"How long?"

"Uh… looks like… 2014."

"My God… four years?"

"Were you… not aware of your mother's condition?"

"We were beginning to suspect, but, no. She's done a good job keeping it from us."

"I'm so sorry. Remarkable she's been able to mask this."

"Yeah. She's something."

Well, the shit's gonna hit the fan now. You can't be incognito anymore, Al. I should have said something sooner. Oh, well, hindsight is foresight as they say.

"David, can you step into the hallway for a second? We'll be right back, Mother!"

"So… Alzheimer's?"

"David... don't jump to conclusions. Even if it's dementia, that doesn't necessarily mean, Alzheimer's. We'll talk with Bennett."

"I still can't wrap my head around it. Ma's so young. I thought only people in their seventies and eighties get Alzheimer's?"

"She is young, David. Early onset begins anywhere before the age of sixty-five, but it does happen in a small percentage of the population. Some people are diagnosed as early as their thirties and forties. Mother probably has what's called, VA, or Vascular Dementia. That means the dementia can cause confusion for a time, and then she can seem normal. It makes it difficult to tell if something's wrong."

"Remember the time she got lost driving, and I picked her up at that woman's house?"

"Yeah, I remember... she missed her exit or something?"

"Right. Meg chewed me out for not taking Ma to the hospital, but I told her she was being ridiculous. I said getting lost was something that could happen to anyone. Ma was shaky, and a little embarrassed, but otherwise, she seemed fine."

"We talked about this David; I might have agreed Meg was jumping the gun. We still wouldn't know Mother was sick, unless we saw her every day, her condition worsened; or if a circumstance cropped up, like this one; getting lost in the basement?

"But Meg warned me. When Ma accused her of stealing? Cripes, that was a dead giveaway. And finding out she hasn't been to church?"

"Yes, David, but we didn't know that until I spoke to Jean."

"But it's my responsibility to know, and if I'd listened to Meg, I would know!"

"We see what we want to see; what our psyches can handle, David. Stop blaming yourself; plus, our information was spread over three people. You were around Mother when she appeared relatively normal, Meg, when Mother was most affected, and I hardly at all."

"But, the puzzle pieces were there."

"David, you need to stop beating yourself up; there's no point, and it's counterproductive. What's most important is what we do going forward. We'll get a full report tomorrow. We can begin the difficult decision-making process then."

"So many little clues... like the fact that she loves t.v., but the last couple of times we watched a movie, she paid no attention; as if the screen wasn't there. I asked her if she was reading any good books, and she complained that they were all boring, and the print was too small."

"David, the two things you just described don't mean a thing. What's unusual about daydreaming while watching television, or not being interested in a book? Come on."

"Ma not interested in any book? That alone should have tipped me off. And I had no idea how dirty the house was."

"No one did, David."

"When, Meg and I wanted to swing by, she'd say she was resting or going to the store. She even said no to a visit from Raine; huge red flag.

My God, Paige, did you smell her? She probably hasn't showered in weeks. Meg was right, I've been in denial. I'm sorry. I'm sorry! This is all my fault. If I had gotten her to the doctors sooner..."

"David? **Stop it! Listen. You are not to blame**. The person we should be upset with is, Mother. She's had this disease for four, five years. Unbelievable. This is typical of her; keeping us at a distance, being secretive and stubborn as hell. What a surprise."

"I'm sure she had her reasons, Paige."

"She's shut us out, David... Robbed us of the last lucid days of her life. There's no good reason for that. Imagine what she's been struggling with; confusion, fear, secrets; trying to juggle medications, tests, doctor's appointments? We could have been here for her; taken care of all these things; and most importantly, spent time with her. Instead, we're scrambling after the fact, hoping it's not the final act.

It's actually embarrassing. Did you see the doctor's face when he realized we didn't know? We shouldn't be the **last ones** to hear about this. I'm a psychotherapist for Christ's sake. There are specialists who...

"Why are you so hard on her, Paige? Not everyone wants to spill their guts. I suspect she didn't want to burden us."

"You're kidding, right? She's impossible. I haven't been able to extract a morsel of meaningful conversation out of that woman in twenty years; believe me, I've tried. We're supposed to be a family, David. Families talk, they share things; difficulties, trials, joys and sorrows; at least that's what functional families do. She should have told us, David. No excuses. Period."

"Paige... Why can't you accept Ma's a private person? You can't force her to be what you need; that's not who she is."

"This goes beyond privacy David, come on! We're lucky she got confused in the cellar, and didn't burn the house down, or wander off one day and freeze to death. And why do you always protect her? She's a grown woman for fuck sakes."

"What do you mean? I don't protect her."

"Yes, you do. Mother bullied you into not taking her to the hospital, and you complied. Why? Meg kept telling you about the warning signs, and instead of investigating, you sheltered her. You and she both in denial, both protecting each other. But, that's how it's always been between you and, Mother, hasn't it? Let's not talk about anything problematic, it might make us uncomfortable."

"And why do you always call her, Mother? It's so... formal, cold.

"I don't know. Because there's always been a chill between us? Anyway, she makes no secret of the fact you're her favourite!"

"You're wrong, Paige. She is so proud of you!"

"Ah, well, being proud of someone's accomplishments and loving them is not the same thing, is it, David?

"You can't honestly believe she doesn't love you?"

"Well, if she does… it's constrained…. controlled. I need more."

"I'm not saying this to hurt you Paige, but if you'd stuck around, you could have worked on the relationship, tried to heal what was broken. You didn't need to go globe trotting. You could have opened a nice practice in town; but it was easier to disappear than deal with the emotional baggage, wasn't it, Paige? I'm not blind, and neither is Ma. You know better than anyone it's easier to fix other people's issues than sort out your own; but you're dead wrong about her not loving you."

"All of this is water under the bridge, because if Ma has Alzheimer's, you'd better sort it out before she disappears."

"It's too late for that David."

"It's never too late."

IT'S NOT HARD TO TRICK YOUR BRAIN

What a fuss, over pickles.

I had a good crop of cukes last year.

Or was it… two years ago? Twenty?

What a mess that first year! I still didn't have a garden, so I bought English cucumbers; skimped on the garlic and salt, and drowned them in vinegar. I didn't have a clue!

And that was when you still had a brain!

All right, no more nastiness!

And fresh dill makes all the difference! I like my pickles to be soft; but not too mushy. Pickling and canning are an art form, and I'm no garden guru. Some women are cooks; some are bakers; and some are show-offs like Martha what's her name? Me? I'm a down-home cook - nothing fancy; comfort food mostly. The more ingredients I can slop into one pot, the better. When the old brain blipped, my crock-pot came in handy. Now… can I remember to eat?

We didn't starve to death, so I'm guessing we derived sustenance somewhere.

I don't know why, but ever since I was a little girl, I've loved pickles. They make me happy; all that juicy tartness. I'm smiling now, aren't I?

Happy… A rather common word, wouldn't you say? What is happiness? A minuscule amount of joy? A congenial sensation? The underdog of feelings? Yet, as unremarkable as it is, I'd give anything to be happy again. I never realized what a blessing joy can be.

Al's gobbled the effervescence; nothing left in that quadrant.

Oh, please. You've never been effervescent in your life! You were always a sour-pussed bitch!

Liar! Remember the year we took the family to Disney World right before Christmas… Or was it, Easter… and there were no lines? **That's happiness!** *I may not feel much anymore, but I still remember I* **did feel**, *once upon a time.*

Semantics.

You might be right. I can't reason things through like I used to; and at this point, it's irrelevant.

"Be joyful in all things," says the Good Book; well, it's what Paul says; but then again, he was a zealot. You think after Christ cleared the cobwebs from his eyes he became a different person? Nah., he went from being Saul, the Christ-hater; to Paul the Christ-lover. He was a fanatic extremist; all he did was switch teams. We are who we are. Pretending to be otherwise is a fool's errand, and disingenuous.

Okay, Popeye! "I yam what I yam an' that's all I yam."

Oh sure, we change our views from time to time; even jump the fence - hell politicians do it all the time. But, at our core we're the same soul, who took our first breath as we entered the world; and we'll be that person when we breathe our last, as we exit.

My brain may shrivel, my memories disappear; Al might make me twitch, stutter, even silence my voice… but I'll still be me.

I'll continue to be who I was before you ever existed, Al, and I will continue to be so long after you're a pile of ash. There's the hope! My soul belongs to God, and no matter what you do, you can't destroy it. I may not remember who I am, but God will recognize me with or without my body, and in the end, I will have forgotten even you, Al! Oh, how I'm looking forward to that!

During a depressive episode, my therapist told me to practice smiling at myself in the mirror. She said while it sounded silly, it would trick my brain into thinking I was happy. It worked. Yes, there were drugs involved; but who's saying smiling didn't contribute?

I remember reading the story of a man who'd lost his hand in a machine accident. The split second before his fingers became mincemeat; he clenched his fist. From that moment, and forever after, his stupid brain clung to the idea that his fist was clenched in a hand that no longer existed. Day after day, the phantom pain tormented him; nails dug deeper and deeper into a non-existent palm. Akin to Chinese water torture; drip, drip, drip; he was in agony, and going mad. He'd seen hundreds of doctors and psychiatrists, to no avail.

Years later, exhausted, and in despair, he decided he'd end it all; but not before seeing one final physician who came up with the ingenious idea of positioning a mirror inside an ordinary container, then asking his patient to put his hand inside the box, fist balled.

"Now, open your hand," he said.

Like magic… the pain was gone. With little effort, he'd tricked the patient's brain into believing the reflection was in fact, the phantom fist.

Genius? The idea, yes; but turns out it's not that hard to trick your brain.

Look in the mirror. Observe. The reflection is an illusion; a falsehood; a twin. We aren't the image we glimpse because the glass only echoes what it sees outwardly. How can it reveal our true self? It's an inanimate object with no emotions, no ability to discern or be introspective. It only shows us what we **look** like; even that's inaccurate because we are actually, a mirror opposite.

We need to rid ourselves of opinions, judgments and doubts, and see ourselves through God's eyes. This doesn't mean lying, it means acknowledging we're not perfect, then working towards self-improvement. Only then can we reflect our true selves.

Contrary to popular belief, it takes tremendous effort for grace to reveal itself.

Take peonies for instance; they wouldn't exist without ants. Resin from the flowers turns into a kind of glue that hardens and keeps the buds from opening. The ants take care of all that goo, by peeling away layer after layer; until a beautiful flower emerges.

I told them I needed ants. Is it too late?

Sorry. Am I rambling? Tangents seem to be par for the course these days.

Anyway... quite a fuss over pickles!

Am I late for the party? Why did you let me prattle on about pickles and peonies when David will be here any minute to pick me up?

Where's my dress?

YOU'RE OKAY, I'M OKAY

"It's alright, Mother. You're okay."

"Where am I?"

"You're in the hospital."

"Where's Baba?... There are ants there."

"It's okay. You've had some tests. Do you remember what happened?"

"I don't need tests... I bumped my chin; that's all."

"Do you remember being lost in the basement? The doctor ...

"NO! No more doctors! Take me home!"

"Okay... okay, Mother... no more doctors."

"I want to go home!"

"I know. We'll find your clothes. We'll get you dressed and…

"Hello, everyone, I'm Doctor Kinney, Dr. Bennett's colleague. I'll be looking after mum while she's here."

"I need ants... Can I go home?"

"Sure. Is this your son and daughter?"

"My car got lost, and I couldn't get to the barrel... They wouldn't give me ants and now… Oh-oh, I forgot rule number one."

"What's rule number one? Oh, don't cry, Ma. Everything will be okay."

"Your mom is still confused, so, it's important to keep her calm. It's helpful if only one person at a time speaks to her, preferably in a quiet space. If there are distractions, she'll find it difficult to follow the conversation. Speak slowly. It takes time for her brain to catch up, so don't expect a quick response. She has to process what's being said before she can respond, so you'll need a lot of patience.

Offer reassurance and encouragement if you find she's struggling. It's going to be difficult, but if she senses you're frustrated, she'll get frustrated too. Most importantly, remember this is still... Mom."

"Why am I in jail? What did I do?"

"Nothing. You did nothing, Ma. Everything is okay. Doctor Kinney wants to be sure you aren't hurt before he sends you home. Okay?"

Liars! They put Kooky Cookie in jail, and that's where I'm going! Don't put me in with that smiling bitch. I'd rather be dead!

"If I'm not in jail, why can't I leave? I want to go home. Can I?"

"Soon, Ma I promise. Someone special is waiting to see you. Can you guess who? I'll give you a hint. She has brown curly hair and big hazel eyes."

"Angela? Is Angela here? Angela has straight hair, and brown eyes. Did she get a new hula-hoop?"

"No, Ma, not Angela. Do you remember Raine's party?"

"No, I don't like parties, and I don't like rain! I want to go home."

"Doctor... Will my mother be confused from here on in?"

"Your mother's disease is progressing. She'll have good and bad days; however, this is the time to consider long-term care. She'll need round-the-clock care from here on in.

If you have any questions, here's my card. You can contact me, or Dr. Bennett at this number. In the meantime, here's a list of LTC facilities you should look at. All the institutions mentioned are excellent and provide outstanding care for Alzheimer's patients. Good Luck... Dr. Bennett will be in touch."

"Can we take her home?"

"We'll give her some medications to make her more comfortable, and then yes, she can go home... Who'll be staying with her?"

"I will!"

"Good. Are you her daughter?"

"Yes."

"If you give me a minute, I'll be right back with some prescriptions. I suspect your mom has these meds at home; make sure they're up to date. If they're past, their efficacy date, it's best to renew."

"Thank you."

"Mother, how are you feeling? Are you comfortable?"

"Paige?"

"Yes... Mother?"

"Are you home from school? There're cookies in the kitchen."

"Mother... we're in the hospital."

"Is it your appendix again? I thought they took that out?"

"No, Mother. Do you remember being in the basement?"

"Yes... I was getting... pickles."

"That's right. But, you couldn't remember how to get upstairs."

"What? Are we in the big house by the park?"

"No, Mother. You live on Collins Street. It's a bungalow with a basement."

"Collins Street?"

"Yes, right across from Beckett's Creek."

"Can I go home?"

"Yes, Ma. Paige and I will take you home."

"Paige? Paige!"

"Yes, Mother, I'm right here."

"I want to tell you something. Come closer."

"What?

"I peed the bed."

"It's okay."

"Shhh, whisper… I don't want, David to hear."

"It's all right, Mother. We'll keep it between us girls. I'll get the nurse to change that for you."

"What's going on, you two?"

"It's our secret, isn't it, Mother?"

"Ma, as soon as you get dressed, you can go home."

"Home? No… I…

"You don't want to go home?"

"I… I do… but…

"Please don't cry, Ma. Everything is okay."

"It's not... okay. I'm sorry. I'm sorry."

"No need to be sorry, Ma."

"I'm sick."

"Don't worry. The doctors...

"Paige? Where is Paige? Paige!"

"Right, here. I'm right here, Mother."

"It's private... I don't want David to hear. He'll be scared, like that time you went to the hospital and had your tonsils out, and he cried because he was afraid you weren't coming home? We need to protect your baby brother."

"Okay Mother, you can tell me. David's not listening."

"... I've... I've never...

"It's okay, you can tell me."

"I'm... sick."

"You are?"

"Yes. I... I have... Al."

"Al?"

"Alz… heimer's."

"Yes, Mother… The doctor told us."

"David too?"

"Yes, David too, and it's okay. Don't worry. We're fine, and so are you. We're going to take care of you... we love you."

"I love you too… both of you. I'm so sorry. I didn't… don't want you to suffer this with me."

"Who took care of us through chicken pox, colds and what not? Hmm? It's our turn. It's what families do; look after each other."

"Forgive me… forgive me if… I can't remember… Ohhhh…."

"Don't cry, Ma."

"Mother, there's nothing to forgive you for."

"The memories… fading… the memories of you… David… everyone.

"It's all right, Mother. Love never fades, and neither will you."

"If I forget… tell, Rainey… I love her."

"Every day, Ma... every day."

I RAISED A BEAUTIFUL GARDEN

Just what makes that little old ant,
think he'll move that rubber tree plant.
Anyone knows an ant, can't move a rubber tree plant...
But he's got high hopes. He's got high hopes.
He's got high apple pie, in the sky hopes.
So, any time you're gettin' low, stead of lettin' go,
just remember that ant and...
Oops, there goes another rubber tree plant.

I was pondering perseverance, given my current circumstance. How long should one trudge on before being considered stubborn? A year? Four? Ten? Consider for a moment, that less than a breath separates genius from insanity; life from death; love from hate? So, what's the difference between perseverance and hope; or resilience for that matter? If you want my two cents, I believe tenacity is ingrained in our DNA. It has a purpose, like our survival instinct. It's not digging one's heels in, or being obtuse or stubborn; while, resilience, is a scholarly discipline; at least it was in my case. I never achieved it, not wholly.

Everyone assumes I'm made of iron, but the truth is I'm flesh and blood like everyone else. I've come apart more times than an unknotted thread.

Am I unravelling now? No. We're okay. We're okay.

Hope? Well, it's the Hail Mary of life. It's the letting go… not directing, not manipulating, merely allowing grace to do its thing.

Now, ants have stick-to-it-iveness; they're all about purpose. Without ants, peonies wouldn't exist. They open the delicate folds by sucking up the moisture on the bud before it hardens. Have I told you this already?

No more struggling… no need for perseverance; resilience all eaten up, but hope?

Jesus loves me still today,
Walking with me on my way,
Wanting as a friend to give
Light and love to all who live.

Peonies are my favourite flower. Many would say, it's just like me to choose a plant that requires work and patience. Ah, but once opened, they're glorious! Have I talked about this before?

People are like flowers. I'm not the only peony; my daughter's one too. She required a lot of patience and hard work, but when she blossomed she was spectacular! Did you know she's a world-renowned psychotherapist? I'm so proud of her; strong, beautiful, talented. We're two peas in a pod. The difference between her opinions and mine, is that her viewpoints are educated and brilliant. Let's leave it at that.

When she was a baby, I would rock her for hours and just watch her sleep; her feathery eyelashes resting on her lower lid; her little breast rising and falling with quick, baby breaths. She looked like an angel. What I wouldn't give to rock her now. Of course, she wouldn't let me; she's not a baby anymore, is she?

Is she?

No, and soon she'll be rocking you!

It's reassuring you're still with me, Al. It means I'm alive. I know you're on the move; march, march, march... ever onward. Soon, I won't hear your voice, and, there'll be... Well, I'm not sure - nothingness? Space... the final frontier? Why is that familiar?

We're all stardust. I read that once... it's comforting knowing I'm part of something bigger than myself.

Sorry. Non sequitur? Um, flowers, yes? No? Babies?

In my Mother's day, they kept you in the hospital for a week after you delivered, so you could rest and recover; let your hormones settle down. Now, they send you home as soon as your placenta falls out. Idiots! Anyway, after a few days, I noticed my little angel looking jaundiced, so back we went.

They put us in a room with a blue gingham rocking chair. I still remember the fabric; such a happy blue. We glided back-and-forth, back and forth, right in front of a lovely window overlooking a park. The clouds floated by like a gaggle of cotton balls, all soft and pink.

When, Paige wasn't in the incubator, blindfolded under a purple haze, I would cuddle her and stare at her itty-bitty nose, and cherry blossomed cheeks; smooth and pudgy. I remember wishing I could stay that way forever; rocking and gliding; cooing and cuddling. Unfortunately, life isn't stagnant, and it moves in one direction.

Not all memories are rainbows and sunshine either, yet, I wouldn't trade them for the happiest ones in the world.

Ah, my, sweet, sweet boy... He was the most delicate flower of them all; a tiny Lisianthus; soft... rare... hard to grow. It only survives days after it's cut from the stem. My delicate flower survived sixty-two days to be exact... Sixty-two of the most unbearable days... then one by one his petals fell until he was... gone. We laid him in a little white coffin; one size fits all. If tears could have revived him, he would be alive; like Lazarus. There were so many tears in the end, but none of them were mine. I was all cried out by then; seven months and sixty-two days worth.

Mommy's coming soon, baby boy.

Nevertheless, resilience, perseverance, and hope all carried me forward. I was talking about that, right? No? Dammit! Sorry. Flowers?

David was my wild ornamental grass. He needed a sunny exposure and pruning from time to time; but otherwise, he weathered wind, rain, snow and ice. Is he a mail carrier? I can't remember.

The question is, will he bend or break in the teeth of Hurricane Al?

Don't you touch him, Al! Don't you ever! I can accept we're going steady, but stay away from my kids!

I named him, David, after the Biblical King because he's always been steadfast, kind, honest and loving; my rock. Oops, maybe I should have called him, Peter? Oh well, too late now.

Everything's too late, isn't it?

What is everything? Life? That ends one way or another - none of us gets out alive. Hope? Well, not for a future here, but I have faith in an alternate existence. I can't conjure what it will be, but I know it's there…

David is a discreet observer. Like the stars, he assimilates, gathers and stockpiles whatever life has to offer and stores it in some secret vault for future reference. There could be no sweeter heart. D is the Gardenia of my garden. When he was a tyke, he crept into my room, and I remember he stroked my head with his peanut-buttered fingers… sang me a little song. Where have those days gone?

Did I say grass, or gardenia? What does it matter? He can be both, can't he? None of us is one dimensional.

Oh, please, you remember shit! And you're rambling!

Why did you kill a tender moment with my son? You're such a base beast, aren't you, Al? And don't think because I've never spoken it, I've forgotten your name. Remember… when I die, so do you. It used to give me such pleasure imagining it. Now,

261

there's... peace, because in the end, I'm not just a brain! I'm **so** much more than what you're destroying!

I was a giver of life, and that's love! Love conquers all, Al. You understand none of that, do you? You're only teeth and tangles, and death.

I raised a beautiful garden. That's what matters. And guess what, Al? I'll be remembered forever through them.

You? You won't be as much as an afterthought.

I HAVE ALZHEIMER'S

I have Alzheimer's.

I wanted to tell you before disease destroys my ability to merge thoughts, complete sentences... and remember. I was diagnosed... eight years ago? But, don't make book on it.

Did I mention I have Alzheimer's? I never dreamed I'd say the word, as if speaking its name, would make it more powerful. Silly, because we're not in control of our brain, or the diseases that attack it, any more than we control whether the sun will shine.

Most days, journeying with Al has been, exhausting and frustrating; and it's taken me years to understand, it wasn't personal. I wasted so much energy fighting an imaginary foe, much like Don Quixote and his windmills.

Why do we cling to the notion we must be courageous? Don't believe me? Read any, obit; fought courageously, battled, went down fighting, paid the ultimate price. I prefer the notices that read, died... peacefully, surrounded by family. That's what I want mine to say.

I've seen those who've struggled against death; gasping, moaning, shouting, clinging. So ugly... so much fear... At least, Al allows for a calm succumbing.

Don't misunderstand. I'm not saying, Al is my friend, but he's also not my enemy. He's a biological disease, programmed to destroy the human brain. Like thousands of other diseases our bodies are prone to, it will rob us of life, but it does so without malice. There's no ill intent.

I won't minimize the damage either; losing one's ability to reason, speak, maintain bodily functions and remember, is frightening. But, as I've said, control is an illusion. Life is chock-full of random events; just ask the guy running to catch the bus who gets struck and killed by a car. A storm fells a tree, you escape, only to step outside on a live wire. Babies die before they've lived; a crazy gunman opens fire, and kills someone with a ricocheting bullet.

People say everything happens for a reason, but a volcano has no motive when it blows its top and kills hundreds of people. I don't think God says, oh-oh, too many people down there, time to cull the humans. However, I don't presume to understand the omniscient mind, so who am I to say how it works?

While humans can be fiercely resilient, we also have fragile psyches. Everything seems fine until one day we wake up, feeling as if we're at the bottom of a well. I can tell you from personal experience, depression serves no purpose. My point is, life is full of random occurrences and disease is one of those things.

I won't weigh in on the whole, food, pollution, exercise, debate, as I have no expertise in these fields, but I will pass along my own philosophy. As long as we live in these fragile shells, they will age, and we will die. If you use and abuse yourself, your body may crumble sooner, but like the vegan jogger who dies of a heart attack or a baby born with tracheoesophageal fistula, (T.E.F.) sometimes there are no answers.

Our genetics are immutable. I hope one day, they can snip Al from the DNA link, along with other maladies that cause suffering; guess we'll just have to wait and see. It's too late for me, but I will do all I can to help the next generation. Yup! I'm leaving the old noggin' to science. It will be of no use to me when I'm gone.

I hope God won't mind me showing up empty-headed. He'll expect it. Did I mention, I'm human? Ha-ha. Brainless, or Al brained is pretty much the same thing. Ha-ha-ha. Anyway, how we die is as important as how we live, perhaps more so; but we must do both, well. We owe it ourselves, and to those we love.

So, I'm at the end of my journey. I hope I mattered, and that I will be… remembered. I pray that my brief time on this planet was spent well, and that I left something of value on the path; kindness, a smile… the good stuff. These revelations are far from unique. I believe those who've gone before me, and those who will follow, also share these desires.

The world won't blink when I depart, but whenever I'm grieved, thought of, or cried over, I will live. Each time my name is mentioned, or someone smiles when they think of me, I'll be there. If a joke I told brings peals of laughter, I'll be remembered. And I know I'll live on in the hearts of my children, even when I cease to recognize them. What more can I ask?

I may be repeating myself, but love… conquers all. Cliché, but true!

SHE CALLED ME MOM

So much busyness! People fly around like they're in one of those revolving things.

Hey… Can you help me get out? I only went for pickles. Or was it, peonies? I must have stolen them because, I'm in prison. They keep telling me I'm not, but I can't get out, so, you do the math.

See that big silver box over there? Shhh. It's a vaporizing chamber; people go in, but never come out.

If it's Hell, Jesus will rescue me. He's coming for me.

Jesus, remember me… I've been a good girl. Please take me to heaven. Remember me, Lord when you come into your kingdom… Remember me… I want to go home. Father, please, bring me home.

I asked for a pickle; but the coming and going pantsuits say, it's breakfast. We're always eating around here. We don't eat pickles; they're not the Breakfast of Champions!

Was that a commercial?

The starship automatons must shop at the same buy one, get one free store; they wear multicoloured, but otherwise identical pantsuits. There must have been a clearance!

Breakfast, then bedtime; repeat, repeat, repeat. The place is run by robots and Stepford wives. Wait. Weren't the Stepford Wives, robots? They're hell's minions for all I know. They never stop talking; always, blah, blah, blah, blah, but I don't listen.

Sometimes, I hear a piano and singing, but it's because I had a brain accident; like a hundred years ago. That's why I'm in jail; brain carnage.

Hmmm, hmmm, hmmm, mmm, mmm, la, la, la. Fweet, weet, weet. Oh-oh. Baba says whistling brings the devil in the house.

Sometimes, Babcha and I hold hands and dance in the backyard, and sometimes we just watch the ants.

That dark-skinned man, in the yellow? He brought me a looking glass, and Snow White's stepmother was in it. She's in the room next to mine. She has gray hair, and whiskers. I wonder why he showed me that? Well, I won't be eating any apples!

The Bible says there'll be a gnashing of teeth, so this can't be Heaven. Besides, judgment won't be handed down by a woman in a puce pantsuit, will it?

I need to go home. Who's going to take care of my peonies? Ants can't do it all by themselves.

A beautiful girl came to see me today. She came out of Heaven's silver box. I think she's an angel.

She called me... Mom.

EULOGY

Thank you all for coming.

Near the end, Mom expressed sorrow at the fact she would have no friends to mourn her when she passed. We assured her this wasn't the case, and if she's looking down at us today, I know she's smiling.

Day by day, hour by hour, this horrible disease, which she referred to early on by many names such as the Great Devourer, and her favourite, Al; not only ravaged her precious memories, it destroyed the parts of her that were vibrant, engaging, bright and fun. But, it couldn't vanquish her spirit, and while her memories of *us* faded, our memories of her never will.

For me, she will always be the smiling face who greeted me when I came home from school; the soft hand caressing my forehead when I was sick. She was chauffeur, cook, cleaning woman, and nursemaid.

She was also my greatest encourager. She would say, "you can do it," no matter what, "it," was.

She taught me to be fierce and loyal; to stand up for my beliefs, even when she knew there were times I would stand alone.

She gave me my love of books; my curiosity about people; a love of rain and trees; sun and moon; stars and God.

She taught me to embrace uncertainty; to live a mindful life, and to always be my authentic self.

We didn't always see eye to eye, but I know she loved me, and as she was wont to say; love conquers all.

She was my comfort, and I feel privileged that in the final stages of her life, she allowed myself, and my brother to be hers.

She was resolute in life, and courageous in death, not because she battled, but because she accepted death with dignity and peace.

We will be planting a hedgerow of peonies along the back wall of the church. I'm sure many of you know they were Mom's favourites. I hope each time you pass them, you remember her.

I would also ask each of you to remember Mom as a caregiver, choir member, helper, the shoulder you cried on, the friend you laughed with; the book maven, movie enthusiast, nature lover, dreamer, stargazer, writer, woman of faith, grandmother and... mother.

Until we meet again... I love you... Mom.

About the author

Kim Drake was born and raised in Toronto and now lives in the greater Ottawa area with her husband, Brad.

She has two grown children; Matthew and Taylor.

Kim has been writing, and storytelling for over forty plus years, and has previously authored a book entitled, CROSS which can be purchased on Amazon.com, or downloaded onto a Kindle; with half the proceeds being donated to Build-On – an organization supporting education across the globe.

https://tinyurl.com/y7db5nq6

Several of her poems have also been published in various poetry anthologies.

Resources

www.alzheimer.ca

www.alz.org

https://www.alzheimers.net

29722378R00175

Made in the USA
Lexington, KY
02 February 2019